EPIPHANY

J.V. Gachs

Sobelo Books

Book Cover by Yorgos Cotronis
Edited by L.C. Marino and L.P. Hernandez
Formatted and published by Sobelo Books

ISBN (paperback): 978-1-965389-22-5
ISBN (ebook): 978-1-965389-21-8

Second edition, 2025

Praise for Epiphany

"J.V. Gach's *Epiphany* is a melodic, gripping and complex modern Spanish fairy tale. I was enchanted and terrified all the same." – **Cynthia Pelayo**, Bram Stoker Award winning author of *Children of Chicago*

"A nightmarish tale rooted in folklore and found footage elements. Gachs is at her best when giving you a look behind the motivations and decisions of those who make bargains with sinister supernatural forces." – **Patrick Barb**, author of *Night of the Witch-Hunter*

"A riveting debut from JV Gachs, Epiphany weaves mystery and Spanish folklore to create an enthralling tale of horror that will stay with you for years. Haunting, heartbreaking, and fiendish, this is a definitive staple of European folk horror." – **Pedro Iniguez**, author of *Echos and Embers* and *Mexicans on the Moon*

To all the girls who craved magic and found monsters instead.

ESTELA

I became a widow the day I heard my baby's heartbeat for the first time.

"Estela, are you alone?" The tone of Jennifer's voice, my wife's co-worker, on the other end of the phone was enough to make my legs tremble.

"No, I'm at the hospital, I'm having my first ultrasound today ... What's up, Jen?"

"Did anyone accompany you?"

"No, Eva should have come, but yesterday she decided she'd rather go with you up north to finish the podcast in a different way. Are you going to tell me what the fuck is going on?"

"I need you to say that you need to go in now to see the doctor and put them on the phone."

I don't blame Jennifer. After all, it couldn't be easy for her to break the news to a pregnant woman that her wife had hanged herself from an oak tree five hundred miles from home when she should have been at her baby's first ultrasound.

The baby she wanted.

I would never have made this decision if not for her. Eva wanted to be a mother more than anything. I just wanted to make her happy. If her attempts to gestate our baby herself had worked, we might not be in this situation now.

As I lay on the stretcher in the ultrasound room, I did not fully comprehend what they were telling me. Death was something abstract. An absurd notion that could not apply to my wife.

"She had an accident, a heart attack?" I asked several times even though I had been given the answer from the beginning.

"I found her. She committed suicide," Jennifer repeated to me, her voice broken, trembling, but patient.

"No, but it can't be. She was going to film the forest today. She said you were going to meet her there. She didn't like the ending you prepared."

"She hanged herself from the oak tree where Coral's brother was found. I-she wasn't answering my calls, so I went to the woods and, I found her, Estela. With the tape recorder at her feet. She recorded everything. I had to be the one to tell you, I couldn't let you find out from a stranger."

Eva would never have taken her own life. Not in those woods, without knowing our baby, without a passive-aggressive good-bye note blaming someone else for her actions? No, that's not, *was* not. Eva's style. Even if the thought of leaving us alone hadn't made her reconsider, the idea that my wife might have killed herself before finishing the podcast she'd been working on for a year was simply absurd. Who risks their marriage, their entire life for a project to hang themselves before seeing it through?

The blow was so devastating it had an anesthetic effect. My mind, my body, decided not to accept anything that was happening. While I was forcing Jennifer to repeat the same thing over and over again, a flurry of staff in white coats took care of me. My tension. My heart. Everything was happening very slowly and so fast that it was impossible to follow. I didn't understand anything they told me. I concentrated on breathing. On blinking. On my heart pumping blood through my veins. As if my body had forgotten how to stay alive and I needed to execute those involuntary actions consciously.

And then I heard it.

An accelerated rhythm. Pink noise with the cadence of the waves that rose above the voices of the nurses, of the gurneys, of the outside world. The ultrasound room ceased to be a confused jumble of voices, needles and white coats.

There was only that sound and me. I let the phone fall out of my hands. Jennifer's concerned voice sounded far away from the receiver. The technician then turned the monitor so I could see my baby's heart contracting. Beating.

A newly formed heart occupying the hole Eva's had just left.

The beat of a new world inside me.

**Excerpt from THE GARDEN OF HORRORS:
A True Crime Company Podcast**

Episode 1, aired on June 2, 2018
[The Bear Dance, acoustic version]

In the folklore of northern Spain there is a particular myth my grandmother used to scare me.

If you don't behave, the xana will come and take you away. She will leave me a xanino who will surely behave better than you.

The xana is an evil fairy, a kind of dryad, who lives along rivers or forests. Some say they were part of the hunting party of the goddess Diana. The xana, for others, is a bewitched lady waiting for love. She does not pursue the love of a companion.

La xana longs to be a mother.

The women in my grandmother's village used to say the xanas went around at night stealing babies and exchanging them with their own offspring. So that the women in the village would nurture and teach them the language of humans. So that they would baptize them.

There are many local variations of the myth, as with all folklore. In certain valleys, the xana would leave a four-peaked loaf of bread for a man to take care of for a full year, at the end of which she would marry him and make him immensely rich *if* he managed to keep the bread intact. Needless to say, the bread was never whole at the end of the story. In some mountains, the xana offered her treasures to whoever would unravel, without cutting the thread, a skein of gold. It is also said that whoever listened to the song of a xana became possessed. They lost their minds forever.

Be that as it may, the core of the myth remains the same: a beautiful lady, a haunted nature spirit, a dark fairy of the forest demanding sacrifices in exchange for treasures. A barren witch willing to do anything to become a mother.

I'm Eva Villar, and this is The Garden of
Horrors, a True Crime Company podcast.

THREE BODIES FOUND IN VALLE DE DIOS
Hospitalized sixteen-year-old girl
sole survivor of horrific crime

12:35 January 7, 2008
Silvia Gallardo

Everything indicates the bodies, in different states of decomposition and not yet officially identified, belong to members of the same family.

The Guardia Civil has confirmed that there is only one survivor. A minor, sixteen years old, who would have been the person to raise the alarm. The young woman is currently recovering in the regional hospital from injuries of varying severity.

Four units of the Guardia Civil, including one from the Unidad Central Operativa, have moved to the house to begin the relevant investigations.

ESTELA

It has been a month since the funeral and there is hardly anything left of Eva at home. We donated her clothes, her mother took some t-shirts, photos, mementos so she could mourn her. I gave books and records to people Eva cared about. But her office is still intact. Full of boxes and dossiers. Her computer. A year of work. Recordings, scripts, notes. Her personal diaries. Jennifer has offered to pick it all up, to release me from the burden of finding something that would hurt me. She doesn't say it, but she thinks it. There has to be the answer to why she did it. On some crumpled piece of paper inside the wastebasket. In a train of thought scribbled in the margins of a script. An e-mail. A lover no one knew about.

Jenni dares not bring up the subject with me in my condition. She feels guilty.

Guilty for not seeing something was going on. Guilty of having believed that supposed joy Eva was brimming with. Guilty for having arrived late to the forest that morning. For not having accompanied Eva to the interviews with Coral.

Nor does she dare to tell me she is afraid for me and for the child. Everyone seems convinced I am going to lose her, or that I will do something crazy, dragged by grief, by this immense pain. But the child is strong, I feel her inside me, and she is not willing to let me off the hook that easily.

Jennifer knows we often argued because of the podcast. I guess she's afraid I'll blame her. She was her best friend; it would be terribly naïve of me to think that my every word during the months she spent visiting Coral at Corazón de María wasn't replayed in voice notes, emails or over coffees while chatting about work. Twisted, of course, to fit her version of the fight. Maybe she thinks those same discussions, tainted with "I knew it" would now be replayed with her. But I know Jennifer had nothing to do with my wife's unbridled enthusiasm.

I've never seen her so involved with a project, and it only got worse when she started interviewing Coral. I'm embarrassed now, but I was jealous. I, with my red hair, my green eyes, my body subjected to a thousand diets and hours of exercise, felt jealous of a young woman locked up for the last ten years. Pale, badly cut hair, unkempt teeth and ...and a past more fascinating than I would ever be.

Eva went all out with the podcast, to the point of not realizing she was neglecting us. Like the time she forgot my mother's birthday and pretended to ask her to make *casadielles* for Coral. Who would ask her mother-in-law to make pastries for a murderer? I'm sure she didn't see it that way, of course.

Jennifer loves me, in spite of everything. We have known each other for over ten years and she knows it was not my fault, nor hers. She offers wholeheartedly to suffer in my place, but I have decided not to accept her offer. We are in no hurry, the little girl growing inside me and I. We have all the time in the world to empty her office ourselves. So, I have decided to do it alone.

I want to be able to get angry with Eva when I find things I don't like, to cry on the floor without anyone feeling the need to comfort me. I want to scream if I feel like it, break things or simply lie in bed hugging the child in my belly and trace my wife's neat handwriting with my shaking fingers. Laugh at her indecipherable Post-it notes.

Understand, why the fuck she hanged herself from a tree and left me alone.

Us.

She left us alone.

I sit on the floor and open the first box marked with a black marker.

Brutos Eva

There's a small mountain of memory cards. I put the laptop on my lap and insert the card with a huge *1* on a red sticker.

Eva appears on the screen. Recording herself in the car. She has curly black hair pulled back in a messy bun. She was never good at taming her curls. Whenever she went to an important event, an interview, even when we had a date, she spent hours straightening her hair. The dark circles under her eyes are evident behind the thick horn-rimmed glasses. It makes my heart shrink to see her so nervous. So willing. With her round little face so full of life. Suddenly, I am struck by her visage within the satin of the coffin. She who never wore make-up, painted like a sad clown. Dead.

I lower the lid of the laptop to catch my breath. I cry until my breath steadies. I open the computer again.

Play.

CLR_IMPRESSIONS_DAY_ONE.mp4

It is January 8, 2018. I am sitting in my car outside the door of the Corazón de María Correctional Center. I couldn't let this unique opportunity slip away. Estela is not at all amused that I'm spending part of our vacation in town researching for the podcast, but she knows how important it is to me. The first interview Coral López Ramos gives, and she gave it to *me*! I guess she thinks it's been long enough. Ten years. A podcast can give her the opportunity to be understood by an audience unfamiliar with her case. Or not at all. As gruesome as the crimes were, for many people they never happened.

It will soon be the 10th anniversary of her conviction, so the timing couldn't be better. I hope this goes well. If it ends up being a bluff, if she has no intention of telling me the truth ... I will have ruined Estela's vacation for nothing. But what if? What if Coral reveals what she really did that day? To me. Could I be the one to find the baby after all this time? And Raúl Expósito?

I will record my impressions of the interviews as we do them. I don't want the tone of each episode to be clouded by the conclusions I draw. I'm afraid my opinion of Coral will change when we get to the murders, and I don't want to be unfair to her version of events.

First impression before entering: I'm ... I'm scared. I'm *very* nervous. It's eight o'clock in the morning. I drove up here late yesterday, got a crappy room and didn't sleep at all. I spent all night going through the case files, to make sure I won't miss anything. I want to give an accurate and in-depth look at what happened in that house. In the woods.

Coral deserves to tell her story, regard-less. She was a minor at the time of the trial, so she was never given the opportunity to do so. Not really.

Coral's doctor will greet me at the door. The building doesn't look as inviting as it does in the pictures, so it might be worth noting that for the listeners. I don't want them to think it's a decent place, like living a hotel, or any of that crap people say sometimes. Actually, it's pretty depressing. The walls are covered with rust stains spilling from metal plates that are so old and dirty you can't even read them anymore. The lawns and trees at the entrance are not at all taken care of. The Corazón de María is old-fashioned and, from the outside, might even look abandoned.

Well, Doc is here.

DOCTORA_MIGUELEZ.mp4

EVA: I'm recording this, okay?

DOCTOR: Yes, of course.

EVA: You were telling me that you don't think this is going to be good for Coral and that you would like to have your opposition on the record in the podcast?

DOCTOR: Yes, this is not good for her. Not good for her at all. I can't object. If I had any kind of decision-making power, you wouldn't have gotten this far. She has the right to give all the interviews she wants, of course. But I've worked with Coral since the day she arrived. She's a stubborn creature, and, in spite of that, we've made progress. We've come a long way. She had already stopped talking about the presence of the oak tree, the baby. And then you started calling. Ten years of work down the toilet with a few calls.

EVA: Well, don't you think she deserves to tell her version of-

DOCTOR: There is not *her version* here. There's the truth, there's the deception, and there's the world Coral created so she wouldn't have to take responsibility for her actions. And that, my dear, is exactly what you are going to feed into with all this podcast guff. If Coral is here, it's because she is still considered a danger to others. But mostly to herself. I hope neither of us have to regret these visits.

CLR_INTERVIEW_DAY_ONE.mp4

[Paper noise]

EVA: I am already recording, Coral. First of all, thank you very much for talking to us. I know it won't be easy for you to remember everything that happened back then.

CORAL: Thank you. This is the first time someone seems really interested in what I have to say. In knowing what really happened. Half the reporters want to interview the merciless killer, and the other half are more willing to believe everything that happened than I am. Well, you know, all those specials on that show that was on TV back then, the one about the UFOs and the poltergeists.

EVA: Ah, yes, "What They Don't Tell Us".

CORAL: That one. I never liked it much. They didn't understand anything. I hope you do. I think we'll get along fine, too.

EVA: I hope so too. Let's get started, shall we?

CORAL: Of course.

EVA: My approach, as I told you when we spoke on the phone, is going to be to start the interviews at the beginning, in quotes, and proceed in order up to today. But, for that to work, we would first have to establish *what* the beginning is. So, is there a particular moment you can point to as the *beginning*? Was there an incident you remember as significant in some way to what ended up happening with your family?

CORAL: Oh, yes, of course. The truth is, I know exactly when it all started. It was Epiphany Eve 2000.

CORAL

When I was eight-years-old, I loved surprises, presents and candy. Epiphany was my favorite holiday of the year. Back then, birthdays were still cool. I had not yet lost my mother. Nor my faith in my father's ability to save me from the darkness. My brother Carlos and I had shared our mother's womb for nine months. I came into the world first. He was born a few minutes later, on the shortest night of the year. Perfect summer solstice twins.

Our mother used to tell us we were destined for great things. We were going to be the brightest stars of them all because of that. Because we wanted nothing to do with the night or the cold. As with so many other things, my mother was wrong.

Every year, on the solstice, the children from the village would come to play at our house. Our dad would dress up as some cartoon character we liked, which obviously changed from birthday to birthday, and mom would bake two huge identical cakes with our names written in candy.

Todos los Santos was my second favorite after Epiphany. It was very different from how Guillermo, my father, remembered it from when he was little, but our grandparents never stopped celebrating it after returning to the old continent. There were lots of candy, spooky decorations and costumes. I loved the sugar skulls our mother made for us and the bright orange marigolds. Our house was the brightest, most cheerful those days. Nothing like the plastic flowers and fake mourning of our neighbors who chose to visit their dead on that day, and only that day, mostly to avoid the poisonous gossip if they didn't parade to the cemetery.

Even the Easter egg decorations, the huevos pintos they call them here, and the treasure hunts were fun, but those celebrations lacked the most important ingredients for me: magic and faith. And Epiphany had plenty to spare.

Good children were rewarded for their impeccable behavior that night, just as our mother had explained happened to the baby Jesus. His birth had been signaled by the brightest star that guided three wise kings from the East across the desert to find the new baby god. There, in Bethlehem, in a sad stable, he was offered three wonderful gifts. I know it's more fashionable now to celebrate Santa Claus, but when I was little, the fat man in red was still more of a movie or commercial character. We would write letters to the Reyes Magos and they would bring what we earned. A pretty simple system. The same as the grades at the end of the school year, but with magic.

On the eve of the fifth of January, there was always a big parade in our town. And also, in every other corner of the planet. Can you believe it? That was the sign of their true powers.

Ubiquity. I learned the word in catechesis. I was probably the only child who paid attention. My brother certainly didn't.

Every fifth of January, hundreds of people from the Far East paraded in front of our house as soon as it got dark. The cohort of the Reyes Magos was colorful, bright and musical. Those men had lived thousands of years and had never failed to fulfill their mission, as far as I knew. It took me years to recognize the baker, the veterinarian. To see the plastic and the glitter of the costumes.

Melchior, Gaspar and Balthazar would throw candy to the excitedly jumping attendees. It was the only time my brother Carlos and I could see the three men up close, because it was strictly forbidden for children to go near them while they were working at night.

The routine in our home was to have an early dinner and go to bed eager for the next morning. Sometimes, there was no sleep at all. Carlos and I had our own rooms, but I would sneak out of mine and crawl into his bed. He liked to pretend it bothered him, but it didn't. He clung to me as much as I clung to him.

During the night, the Reyes Magos would leave us colorful gifts magically delivered. Marisa, whom I still called *Mom* at the age of eight, would prepare hot chocolate and homemade golden churros for breakfast and the day was PERFECT.

Such had been my first seven Christmases.

On the eighth, I was determined to meet the Reyes Magos. Of course, I didn't mention it to my parents or my brother. As nice and funny as Carlos was as a child, he didn't know how to keep his mouth shut. He would spill the beans as soon as he met an adult.

Had I told him, would our lives have been different? Could I have saved my family from a horrible death just by telling my brother to meet the Reyes Magos with me?

Maybe, but, at that time, the only thing that mattered was they would try to stop me if Carlos told anyone. They would force me to stay in my room. Lock the door from the outside if necessary. My fevered childhood imagination even pictured my parents tying me to the bed to keep me from getting up. I swear I could even feel the rope rubbing, cutting, burning against my bare skin when I thought about telling them. I was sure that would happen because, every year, Marisa and Guillermo sat with us and gave us *the talk*.

"And remember, children, the Reyes Magos are very good, but only with well-behaved children. If you get up and catch them in the kitchen, they will be very angry," Marisa said year after year like a broken record.

Lies work best when they are based on repetition, you know?

"And they would never leave any presents under the tree again. It wouldn't be just tonight, it would be NEVER AGAIN," added Guillermo.

Other kids in our neighborhood had real Christmas trees in their living rooms. Big ones. Alive ones. But our mother considered it a cruelty to the trees to uproot them just to let them die indoors. Same reason we didn't own a puppy or a kitten. Not until la xana gave me Señor Magia and Carlos' jealousy made Mimi appear.

Marisa did not eat meat either. We did, because the pediatrician was very concerned about our mother imposing her diet on us, and so was Guillermo. One more of the many things they disagreed on. Our father enjoyed fatty bloody cutlets, lamb ribs and even stewed veal hearts, because he said it was nothing more than a muscle, that it tasted strong like liver, but tender. However, Marisa could not help it. She pitied every living thing on the planet to the point she almost lived on broccoli and asparagus alone. It was painful for her to walk past the meat displays at Christmas.

"Poor babies ..." she muttered in front of the lambs and piglets.

According to her, the Reyes Magos didn't care that our tree was fake. Or the fact that we had to put it on the kitchen table because it was even smaller than our TV. The only thing the Reyes Magos cared about was the children's good record. Mine, I was quite proud of.

When I was little, I never punched my brother when he was annoying and, believe me, there were times I felt like sending him to the moon. That feeling never went away, honestly, and at some point, I just couldn't take it anymore. Although you already know that. But, well, back then, the Reyes Magos were watching over us. Whenever our elderly neighbor needed help reading her gossip magazines, I would volunteer and sit next to her at the kitchen table, enduring the smell of cat urine from her nightgown with a big smile, no matter how my stomach churned and my nostrils protested. I made my bed, did my homework, my chores, and sometimes my brother's too. Just in case having one naughty child in the house sent us straight to the blacklist for the year. I made sure everything was in order.

The Reyes Magos were also grateful that the children left them milk, brandy and cookies to enjoy while they worked. Not to be forgotten was a good bucket of fresh water for the camels and, again, not to disturb them while they placed the gifts under the tree.

But my parents had nothing to worry about, I wasn't going to bother them. I was going to give them a thank-you card on which I had drawn in full color the portraits of Melchior, Gaspar and Balthazar. I had painted it the night of January seventh of the previous Christmas, with the thirty-two colored pencils they had given me. The card waited hidden under my bed for a whole year, while I planned the mission to deliver it. If the grown-ups didn't allow the children to approach the Reyes Magos on the one night they were flesh and blood, that could only mean one thing: no one ever thanked them. If being polite was what it was all about, the adults were not doing it right.

That Christmas, when our parents went to bed, my heart beating like a tambourine and my mouth dry, I left my room without slippers, silent as I imagined cats to be, with the letter carefully tucked into my dinosaur pajama pants. The cardboard was cold against my belly. The icy ground stabbed at my feet. I pressed on, ignoring everything my body was experiencing. Enduring discomfort was going to give extra points to my effort when it came time to meet the Reyes Magos. As if, like them, I too had crossed mountains and deserts to reach my destination.

In the kitchen, I sat under the table. The orange light from the streetlamps coming through the window and the smell of vanilla hanging in the air after baking cookies for visitors melt into my memories. Betrayal, to me, tastes like vanilla ever since. It is cold and orange.

The milk and brandy for the Reyes Magos from the East were there, over my head. I had imagined that moment a thousand times in the last three hundred and sixty-four days. Unfortunately, I didn't get it right. Not even close.

The door to my parents' room inched open. My heart plummeted as if thrown from a skyscraper. I was going to be discovered. Punished. I would be dragged out of my hiding place, screaming and kicking and digging my fingernails into the floor until they chipped and painted thin red lines on the tiles. I made myself as small as I could under the table, clutching my knees to my chest. I had never been so terrified. My heart was pounding so hard I was sure they could hear it, that the whole floor of the house was shaking in sync with me. Fear would give me away.

The rustling of the wrapping paper and the muffled laughter was louder than the blood that throbbed rabidly in my temples. With the lights off, Marisa and Guillermo entered the kitchen. I gritted my teeth so hard it hurt. They, who always scolded me for going barefoot, went without slippers. My mother poured the milk and brandy into the sink and emptied the bucket for the camels.

"Not the brandy, dammit, Mar," Guillermo whispered, feigning annoyance. "I wanted a shot of that."

"Oh, come on, it's the cheap kind. The one that came in the Christmas basket from your job," Marisa mocked.

I held my breath. The crunch of crackers filled the room as some crumbs fell next to my father's bare feet.

"Guille, you've already brushed your teeth, you're worse than the children," complained Marisa, taking the plate from him and returning the remaining cookies to the jar.

"It's your fault; they are irresistible, my love, like you." He held her by the waist and kissed her slowly.

Then, the rustling of the paper stopped. Tears of madness and betrayal burst in my eyes like a storm. I pressed my hands against my mouth to muffle the moans.

"They're going to love them," whispered my father.

Marisa's feet approached his, with the sound of a kiss, just before they left the kitchen. Their door closed and the night returned to its former silence and gloom.

Suddenly, it was freezing. The rain pounded on the windows. Or that's how I remember it. It couldn't be true. I stayed hidden under the table for quite a while, long after my parents' door closed. With my eyes shut, I wanted to turn back time. I know it sounds stupid now, but I was sure that the world would be upside down. That when I opened them, the house would be devastated, completely destroyed. Broken tiles, moldy wood, water running down fungus-covered walls. I tried to swallow my fear and anger, but my mouth was a dry sponge. I put my hands to my face and slowly touched myself to make sure I was still there, before gathering the strength to open my eyes and face my new reality.

But everything remained the same.

Not a speck of the world around me moved a millimeter to mourn the world that had just been destroyed. I found that even more insulting. How dare reality carry on as if nothing had happened? I came out of my hiding place and looked at the treacherous gifts on the table. Had we been fooled? All this time? How could it be? Were all the adults in the world in a conspiracy to deceive children?

I had to make sure, so I opened the largest package, which had my name written in bright pink and gold letters.

I had asked for a puppy.

The Reyes Magos would have brought me a puppy.

I'd been so good. Why else but for the promise of a puppy would I have read gossip to the stinky old woman? Or been nice to the stupid teachers? The feeling of betrayal made my stomach twinge and turn. I suppressed a retch.

But yes, there it was. Living proof that I had been played. A small Russian hamster was asleep on a cotton ball inside a cage with the floor covered in sawdust. Were my parents trying to make me believe one hamster was more than enough pay for all I did? Nausea filled my mouth with a bitter taste again, but I didn't make a sound.

Magic existed. That was an indisputable fact. I had felt it in my bones for as long as I could remember. Every cell in my body tingled with certainty. Light was visible, magic was too. And it was everywhere.

If I had been taught what the women in my father's family knew, everything would have changed that night. If I had not been deprived of the knowledge I deserved, my childhood, my life and the lives of those around me would have been very different. But that night, alone in the darkness of my parents' betrayal, there was only one explanation for my little mind. The Reyes Magos were so busy that when they came upon a house already full of presents, they said, "Why bother, less work!" My parents were ruthless adults who manipulated us. But I could reverse that. I could bring magic back into our home and get us off the blacklist.

I opened the cage door slowly and took the hamster in my hands. The animal stood up on its hind legs, trying to make itself bigger, more menacing, but in truth it only succeeded in looking adorable. If I hadn't a vital task ahead of me, I would have spent the rest of the night petting it and playing. He wiggled his whiskers to sniff my hands. He made me laugh with soft quiet giggles.

I put on my yellow boots and matching raincoat and slipped quietly into the courtyard. I still remember how cold it was that night, the icy wind that cut my cheeks, making my lips dry and chapped, my eyes watery. Little ghosts fled my mouth with every breath. I walked down the cobblestone street of my childhood, moving fast, hoping no one would see me even though I probably looked like a firefly floating above the night. Everyone was fast asleep waiting for the Reyes. The hamster and thank-you card traveled tight against my chest. It seemed like I had been walking forever when I finally reached the end of the street, where the forest began.

It was not a huge forest. To be fair, none of the adults called it that. It was just a small piece of forgotten nature, stranded between roads and houses. We lived surrounded by real forests, more lush places, rivers, waterfalls. There were green meadows where only a few animals grazed. Mountains with snow-capped peaks all year round. However, that little redoubt of nature lost among the new houses refused to die. The few oak trees untouched by people were swollen with age, their branches twisting toward the sun like basking snakes. No more than a dozen. They were wise and sacred to a girl like me. It was a magical kingdom adapted to my size. Perhaps because no one but me ever visited them, I could imagine it was mine alone.

No one told me to keep my distance. No one knew what was hiding there, posing as a normal tree, waiting, keeping the others alive, sustaining an eternal spring. The valley was tinged with ochers and golds, with reds and dark greens, only to be stripped bare with the coming of winter. But my forest never lost the bright green of the first spring days. The trunks of the oak trees were so wide that I believed I would need my brother's and my two cousins' outstretched arms to help me encircle them. I never saw an acorn hanging from their branches, nor the ground. Beautiful, but unable to bear fruit.

A firm believer in magic, I never questioned the reality or the motives of this nature that refused to accept the passage of time like other living beings. I never thought it was a trap. A beautiful carnivorous flower wide open.

Waiting.

Longing for the day someone would cross the broken and rickety fence with a wish.

Just like I did that night. An eight-year-old girl desperate and willing to offer anything in exchange for a little magic.

I went a few meters into the forest, where the orange light of the street lamps still reached me. I didn't have the courage to venture further. I had been here many times before when I got angry with Carlos and needed to hit something so I wouldn't hit him. I cried here when the girls at school had told me they didn't want me to play with them anymore. I made friends with the squirrels then. They were quite a bit more fun. I had imagined being a fairy and felt that magic was stronger in the air. I could almost taste it in my mouth. Salty. Bitter. Magic is indistinguishable from bile.

My stupid plan made even more sense now that I had reached the oldest oak tree. Its trunk was so wide that I could not fully embrace it. Its top melted into the sky. It cheered me up. Something like a voice through the branches came to me as clear as the warmth of the hamster in my hands. The oak tree embraced me. It all made sense. The power around me was intoxicating. My head was spinning. I became the perfect ripe fruit that night, and I volunteered to be harvested.

"Tomorrow we'll meet again, okay? By then you'll be a magical and wonderful puppy. I'll call you ... Señor Magia," I whispered into the hamster's little ear.

Then, with my eyes closed I squeezed the pet tightly in my fist, as I had seen my grandmother do with pigeons for rice. Trapping its chest. The animal resisted, fighting for air. Its tiny claws scratched at my palm like needles. Its teeth tried to hurt me enough to make me let go. I endured the stinging pain. I kept repeating to myself what Güelita used to tell me: no sufren, no sufren, no sufren. She always repeated to Marisa's protests that it was a sweet death. Compassionate. Like stepping into a hot bath. She also said no life was wasted. Never. It just came back as an improved version. To keep learning. Until one's soul was so perfect it never needed to come back. I just wanted to help my hamster get better, you know?

The animal finally gave in and stopped moving. I opened my hand. Its lifeless little body looked like an empty sock fresh out of the dryer. Soft. Still warm. The fur stained with my blood. I kissed him, dug a small hole, tucked the hamster inside, covered him back up, and nailed the thank-you card asking for a puppy as a tombstone.

A tiny tomb.

Cardboard.

Colored.

It was a miracle no one noticed my absence. That only increased my confidence in the existence of an ancient magic watching over me.

I didn't sleep a wink for hours. However, the emotions of the night finally got to me. In the gray light of dawn, my body finally gave out, dragging my mind with it. A haunting voice, a distant lullaby, like a wailing woman singing in the woods disturbed my dreams. She sang a story of love and loss I was too young to understand.

I woke up covered in sweat in my bed when I heard movement and voices in the kitchen. I ran downstairs barefoot. My parents were arguing quietly. I couldn't help but see my mother's stunned face. My father was bent over, looking under the refrigerator.

"The Reyes Magos brought you a hamster, but it ran away!" Carlos shouted with a chocolate-stained face, a churro in one hand and a yellow toy tractor in the other.

"We're so sorry, honey, the Reyes must not have closed the cage properly yesterday," said my mother as she kissed my forehead.

"I'm pretty sure those wise gentlemen locked the cage perfectly," my father replied in annoyance. "Don't worry, tomorrow we'll go to the mall and buy you one."

"It's all right."

I smiled and sat down next to Carlos. He had only left me two churros. I was hungry after my late-night walk, but I didn't complain or punch him. The sacred contract with the Magos to be good was still in effect until proven otherwise.

As soon as breakfast was over, I retraced my steps to the forest. The card was gone. A good sign. I knelt. Filled with doubt, I began to dig up the grave, praying my mission would be a success. I hadn't dug out the third handful of dirt when bright, happy eyes looked up at me from the hamster's grave.

"The Reyes Magos! He was there in the forest, we can keep him, can't we, Dad?" I asked almost breathlessly as I appeared in the doorway holding the puppy covered in dirt.

Magic existed. My Señor Magia existed. I knew it and I had proven it. If only to myself. I wasn't going to reveal my new knowledge to anyone. It was my secret. I would finally have something that was mine, and mine alone.

"Yes, well, I guess so?" Guillermo answered hesitantly, looking at Marisa who shrugged her shoulders.

ESTELA

I remember that day. Eva called me right after the interview. She was very excited. She told me it was much more intense than expected. She knew the details of the case; she knew all the magic stuff and so on. But it was one thing to read about it and another thing entirely to hear her tell it. To notice how sure she was, how vivid her memories were.

"I can empathize to some extent with the fact that a little girl with an immense imagination finds a puppy in the forest and thinks it was something magical. I wanted magic to exist when I was little, too," she said, confused.

"Mi vida, that woman is no longer a child. If she continues to believe these things maybe the doctor is right, and you should not continue with this."

She was silent for a moment. I wanted to think Eva was reflecting on my words. That, maybe, for once, she would listen to me. That she would turn around and forget the whole podcast story.

But she wasn't. She was silent because she was *not* listening to me. Eva kept talking as if I wasn't on the other end of the phone. She just wanted to hear her thoughts out loud.

"You know, Coral looks nothing like her teenage pictures. I don't think there's anything left of that girl staring blankly during the trial. The one we've seen these past few months while preparing for the interview. She's too skinny for her build, her hair is so short now. She is the spitting image of her aunt Olvido when she was her age, from the photos I've seen. Dull and gray, yes, like a flower locked up without light."

"Eva, I don't know if …" I wanted to interrupt her, to change the subject. I was uncomfortable with her work, with her talking like that about a murderer. About someone who killed her whole family. Her own baby. We were trying to become mothers. My body was full of hormones to achieve it even back then. So many sacrifices to give life. And Coral was cold-blooded enough to smother her newborn baby with her own hands and do who knows what with the body. And yet she seemed to … like her. I knew Eva perfectly. I knew when someone caught her eye. When she was captivated.

"When she moves, she is so confident, just like her voice. There's something about her. I can't describe it. But it's important I include this in the script of the podcast, don't you think?"

She didn't wait for me to answer before she kept talking.

"How nice and sweet she is. Even for someone like me, so traumatized by all the coverage that was made of the case, if I have to be honest? I mean. I had a hard time setting foot in the woods in my own city after watching late-night specials about her. And yet, knowing everything she did *in detail*, today I enjoyed listening to her tell her story in her own words."

I should have pushed her harder. All my alarm bells should have gone off. But I didn't want to be the cliché of the jealous woman who gets in the way of her partner's career.

I gave in on so many things to see her happy.

"Estela, for a moment, I forgot where we were. It wasn't the yellowish white table and uncomfortable chairs where we were sitting. The fluorescents weren't flickering or cold, like the light in a dental office or hospital. There was no doctor two tables away, watching us. It was just the two of us. Sitting on a blanket of grass with red ants crawling up our legs and birds glaring. Her voice filled the whole space. That voice. I could almost hear the wind through the forest, with the sun streaming through the gaps in the leaves warming our skin."

I didn't know how to answer. I just said goodbye and burst into tears. I should have trusted my instinct, the knot in my stomach when she talked like that. I should have ended it between them.

GUARDIA CIVIL FINDS THE BODY OF THE MISSING BROTHER

With this latest victim, the body count in the Garden of Horrors now stands at four.

15:54 January 14, 2008
Silvia Gallardo

The lifeless body of Carlos López Ramos was found half buried under an oak tree in a forest yesterday afternoon. The cause of death is unknown.

The alleged murderer reportedly confessed the whereabouts of the body of her brother, also a minor.

The Guardia Civil is continuing investigations to determine the cause of death of the four family members.

They are also trying to locate the whereabouts of the baby that the alleged murderer gave birth to on the day the terrible fate of the López Ramos family became known, as well as the baby's father.

Sources of the investigation point out that the minor could have also con-fessed to the murder of her daughter's father. The search in the garden of the property will continue for the next few days.

CLR_INTERVIEW_DAY_TWO.mp4

EVA: Last week we set up the moment you think started it all for you, when you found out your parents had lied about the Reyes Magos, and we ended the session talking about your dog, Señor Magia. The puppy you found in the woods.

CORAL: I did not find it.

EVA: I'm sorry. You're right. The puppy the oak gave you. I'm sorry. You hadn't met la xana at that time?

CORAL: No, and I didn't see her until many years later. It was after I bled for the first time, after I met Raúl Expósito.

EVA: Okay. Well let's skip that for now, then. I know the dog played a role in the trial, but the truth is they couldn't find the remains of any dog on the property. They assume it ran away when all hell broke loose. Well, you know. What happened that morning. But what they did find was the body of a cat buried in a piece of cloth inside a shoebox

when they were digging up the garden
looking for the body of Raúl Expósito,
your literature teacher. Can you tell me
more about Señor Magia and what he meant
to you? And the family kitty? I thought
your mother didn't want to have pets,
it was a big effort for her to consent
to give you a hamster, but you ended up
having two.

CORAL: Señor Magia was a good dog ...

CORAL

His coat was dark chocolate brown, and his eyes were big and goofy. He was smart, loyal and playful. Wherever I went, there he was too. Following me. Protecting me. Marisa and Guillermo made me promise to take care of the puppy. It was to be my responsibility and mine alone. But it was never a burden. Not at all. I loved Señor Magia more than any other living being. More than my parents. Soon enough, more than my brother, too.

I got up every day at half past five in the morning, before going to school, to take Señor Magia for a long walk in the forest where he was born. I fed him, bathed him and took care of his needs. I even taught him a few tricks. Not that I had to try very hard. He understood my every word. It was more like a conversation than training.

Those morning walks in the woods were our favorite time of the day. There I really felt like myself. And it was obvious that Señor Magia did too. My dog chased small birds and squirrels that had no fear of him. He ate tall green grass. He played in the mud. We were free, wild, stray children for a couple of hours before the school bus came, taming us with its honking horn.

Under the branches of the old oak tree, I was protected. As if it was a glass dome that would not allow anything bad to happen. The air was warmer, sweeter, the light golden, even in the deepest winter mornings. If I put my ear close to the trunk of the oak tree, I could almost hear a heartbeat. A distant drum that sang of ancient times. A pulse of life and magic. Returning to the world was like stepping out of my real self into a cold gray mirror.

I was too young to dwell on what was going on there. I was only glad that the magic was real. The Reyes Magos, the Ratoncito Pérez, the xanas, the Nuberu. All the magical creatures were real. They told us all those folk tales. We were expected to believe them. Why should I feel any other way than calm? Of course, even among those magical beings, some were evil. Light needs darkness to shine. They used to tell me when they told me those stories. But what never occurred to me was that they could not be distinguished from the good ones. That evil could be passed off as beauty, as happiness, as understanding.

Evil doesn't feel good, does it?

Any young child you ask to draw an evil or dangerous forest will use dark colors, browns, blacks, strident reds. Perhaps, the yellow of a full moon sneaking through dry branches. They will not paint a blanket of green grass dotted with daisies and dandelions, with leafy trees, butterflies, squirrels and colorful birds. My forest was the perfect world where any child would want to live.

Despite my parents' best efforts, my dog would run to school behind the bus to be with me.

"One day he will be run over, and then I don't want to see you cry about it," Marisa scolded me, but I knew that Señor Magia would never be hit by a car, because he was not just any dog.

Our village was so small we had no school of our own. We took the bus to the neighboring village and its school of a single classroom and children a myriad of ages crammed within.

Señor Magia waited for lessons to end, dozing in the school-yard. All the children loved Señor Magia. It became a morning ritual to greet my magic dog as we got off the bus.

The puppy loved the attention and wagged his tail and drooled all over us happily. But he was not interested in adults at all. He would only acknowledge their presence if it was obvious they were going to get mad at me if he didn't do what they said. He obeyed them but never showed affection.

My parents were concerned that Señor Magia seemed to have a slight dislike for Carlos. They never mentioned it, but the tension beneath their gaze was palpable.

Carlos longed for Señor Magia to love him, as any child his age would wish when a puppy appears at home. Now I understand. I didn't then. My dog behaved as if my brother was invisible. He wouldn't even accept food from his hands. Señor Magia would only eat what Carlos offered if Carlos put it on the floor and walked away or passed it to me so I could give it to him. It made me feel special. Better than him. More deserving of love.

I think Marisa was heartbroken to see her son trying so hard and getting nothing in return, because she went against all her principles and came home one day with a big cardboard box and a bright smile lighting up her face.

I remember how beautiful she looked that afternoon because it was the first time a pang of sadness pierced my heart realizing I wasn't like her. I looked more like my father's family. Rounder, darker, with a wider face and thinner lips. I longed for that beauty I didn't possess, even though I should have. And I hated her for it. As if it had been her choice not to give it to me. Carlos did look like her. We had shared her womb, and it wasn't fair.

"Hey, nenos, come see me in the living room. Nena, put the leash on Señor Magia, please, honey," she told me.

When we were all seated together on the couch, she placed the box on the floor in front of Carlos. It seemed light, and began to move, startling him. He was always a coward.

"Come on, baby, open it, I promise it won't bite. At least, I hope so." she laughed looking at Guillermo.

I sat back down holding Señor Magia, who must have sensed something he didn't like in the box, because he grunted slowly, and only stopped when I gave him a disapproving look and pulled on the leash.

Carlos hesitated.

The box meowed.

Then, completely excited, he almost tore the carton apart with his small, nervous hands. A ball of white fur sat in the center of the box. The kitten was small, fluffy and had big, round blue eyes. It was completely white, except for one black ear. Carlos sighed and took the kitten in his hands, holding it close to his chest. As soon as the animal felt Carlos' warmth, it began to purr. Very loudly. So loud it made the whole family laugh. Even me. It was, judging from the outside, love at first sight on both sides.

"What are you going to call her, son?" asked Guillermo.

"Mimi!" Carlos shouted almost in tears. It was obvious he had been thinking about having his own pet for a long time. I felt a little sorry for him. I had no idea he had been daydreaming about being as loved as I was.

Mimi was to be Carlos' responsibility as Señor Magia was mine. He was expected to be as diligent as I was. We all agreed on that. He was happy to feel like an adult. I know that for a fact. Caring for someone who depended on him and loved him. We are nothing more than creatures who crave love above all else and are willing to do terrible things to get it or keep it.

The first few weeks, the new kitty made some clumsy attempts to play with Señor Magia, to sleep in his warm chocolate fur, but my dog didn't appreciate the company. My brother's cat was stubborn, but she was no dummy either, so she soon stopped trying. There was balance and happiness in the house for a while.

But doubt had taken hold of me since I discovered my parents' betrayal. What else were they lying to me about? I began to question everything they said. After all, they were liars who had tried to deprive me of magic. If I was still pretending to be a good girl, it was only because, as far as I was concerned, my contract with the Reyes Magos was still valid.

One morning, over breakfast, it occurred to me that their treason was so unforgivable they should be deposed, deprived of all their titles.

"Could you pass me the cereal, *Marisa*?" I asked in the most formal voice I could, which seemed to startle my mother.

"Shouldn't you call me *mamá*, nena?"

"Isn't your name Marisa? Everyone calls you Marisa. Guillermo calls you Mar," I answered, as if it were obvious.

"Well, *papá* calls me Mar, yes, but–"

"But what, don't you like your name?" I asked, putting the spoon on the table and looking my mother in the eye. I straightened my posture and placed my hands in my lap, tilting my head slightly to one side. It was my well-choreographed battle against her. I didn't want this to seem less vital to her than it did to me. Marisa hesitated, took a sip of her soy latte and passed me the cereal.

"You know what? Actually, I love my name. It's your grandmother's name too and you should use it if you feel like it."

I smiled. I won a battle. They tried to take something from me, and I had done the same to them. I would never refer to my parents by anything other than their first name after that breakfast. Not even nicknames. No affectionate names. From that moment on they were simply Marisa and Guillermo. Just two regular people who happened to give me house and food. Their love was no better than sour milk on my tongue. Not only did I not want it, but it repulsed me.

ESTELA

Yesterday, I spent the whole night on the floor of Eva's office with my laptop on my knees. Becoming a voyeur of her interviews with Coral. Trying to understand the fascination. At times, it was as if I had left the office and was sitting in Eva's place, in front of a self-confessed murderer who spoke of magic without flinching.

When my back started to kill me, I put the computer down and lay on the bed, on my side of the bed, unable to fall asleep. My head was spinning trying to assimilate the idea that Eva was gone. That she will never come back.

Stroking my bulging belly, I was overcome with an immense rage.

It was not my idea to have this child. I didn't want to be pregnant. To subject my body to these irreversible changes. The skin on my belly tightens, and cracks opening stretch marks that will stay there forever. My swollen breasts will never regain their shape. But she was so insistent. She was so devastated the first attempts didn't work out. That her body rejected what she coveted. I could never see her suffer. And suffer she did. I had never seen anyone cry like when she woke with menstrual blood staining her pajamas. How could I deny her need if she was the love of my life? I accepted, knowing I shouldn't have.

But something changed while she recorded the podcast. Will I be able to discern, in the recordings, the exact moment her mind took a turn? She was convinced this time would be the one. On all the previous attempts she had been anxious, nervous, grumpy. Not only when she had been the one pumping her body full of hormones. In mine, too. She was watching me. No, she was studying me, searching for some detail that would reveal whether it had worked or not. She fondled my breasts but was only looking for changes in them. This time, she didn't do any of that. She was unnervingly calm.

"I knew it," she said, squeezing my hand as the doctor confirmed what the test told us.

I didn't feel anything. I didn't feel any different.

"I've been to the herbalist, amor. I've brought you this to make you and the girl super strong."

"The girl? Eva, but we don't know yet–"

"Oh, yes, I do know. But it's a secret," she replied, winking at me and holding out a jar full of dried herbs.

"What is this?"

"An infusion the women in my family used to drink. My mother had the recipe written down and I passed it on to the lady at the herbalist's shop."

I opened the jar.

It smelled of damp earth. Like rain. Not mint, not chamomile. The herbs were brownish and black. Eva prepared a tea for me. I took a sip, convinced it would taste horrible. But it didn't, it was sweet with a touch of bitterness at the end. My body vibrated as the warm liquid went down my throat. The more gulps I took, the more my body relaxed like floating over the waves in the ocean. I was overcome with the feeling that everything would be all right. That my doubts would be dispelled. That we would be happy forever. There's still half the jar left, and I still make those teas after I eat. They remind me she cared about me.

That she cared about *us*.

And now she left me? She left me alone with the baby she wanted after convincing me our life would be perfect. Like an advertisement for paper towels. A little girl who stains herself preparing breakfast for her mother. And everyone laughs as they clean up the mess.

Lying in bed, after having spent the night diving into the recordings of her research, I hated her so much for taking that away from me. For bringing me back to the reality of my doubts, of heartbreak, of loneliness.

This morning, I woke up with red eyes. My throat dry and sore as if I had spent the night screaming. My body was heavy. I went to the living room, where her ashes were still waiting to be scattered in the sea of her childhood.

They are now hidden in the top cupboard in the kitchen. Between the waffle iron and the Tupperware.

FROM: martagc@mgschool.com
TO: evavillar@truepod.com

SUBJECT: Re: Interview podcast True Crime Company

How dare you?

How dare you ask for this?

That bitch killed our mother, what do you expect us to say about that? We thought our mother had abandoned us, and that was horrible enough for two little girls. Can you even begin to imagine how we felt when our father sat us down in the living room to tell us that our mother had been dead for years? Murdered by her own niece? No, of course you can't, or you wouldn't be trying to contact me and my sister. Do you have any idea what the reporters put us through? What it felt like to answer those stupid questions about the damn dog over and over and over and over again? To face her during the trial? I hope she rots in hell.

And, for the record, I think what you are doing is disgusting.

CLR_INTERVIEW_DAY_THREE.mp4

EVA: Okay, Coral, I think we have avoided the subject enough, and it is time to talk about your aunt Olvido. Your cousins declined my offer to give their version of what happened, just so you know.

CORAL: You shouldn't have asked them.

EVA: Yes, Marta has made it quite clear to me.

CORAL: Don't be like the others.

EVA: What do you mean?

CORAL: Like the other journalists. I may have been cooped up here for ten years, but we have TV, you know? And a library. I've seen everything. I've read everything. Even that awful movie they made. Have you seen it?

EVA: Yes. It's not very good, is it?

CORAL: No, and what about the scene with the-

EVA: Oh, no, yes with the, ugh. No. [Both laugh.] I won't contact them again, relax. You said at the trial, several times, if I'm not mistaken, that your Aunt Olvido was a witch. So was your grandmother, and it was precisely that family legacy what made you interesting to the oak spirit. Did you always know that, or did you suspect it? Was it something your family talked about? When did you first become aware that you had magical abilities? I'm sorry, but I have a lot of questions about this, as I imagine people listening to the podcast will have. It was part of what made the press go crazy.

CORAL: I know, but I'm afraid only a handful of people believed me. My lawyer wanted it that way, he thought our best chance was a result of ... disability. To answer your questions, it wasn't long after my first encounter with magic that I found out they were witches. It was actually the following Christmas.

CORAL

On our ninth Christmas Eve, there was a big family dinner. Instead of the usual four diners, there were to be seven of us. Our aunt Olvido, recently separated, was visiting for the holidays with her two daughters, Marta and Margarita. They were just six and seven years old. Not so small compared to us, but it was a significant gap.

In the days leading up to the vacations, I overheard a conversation between my parents about Aunt Olvido and Uncle Luis.

"Well, we can't blame him, can we? If she goes on with all that witchy nonsense, he's going to drive him away for good. And it's not good for the girls either. Imagine if she did that around our daughter. You wouldn't be happy."

My interest in my aunt skyrocketed at that instant.

"I know, I know. But I'm worried, Mar. Olvi needs help. I don't want her to end up like our mother. It would break my heart to lose her as well," Guillermo answered with a trembling voice I had never heard before. His voice broke and he cried as

Marisa hugged him. It was the first time I had seen my father cry. I supposed he had cried when my grandparents died, but I was just a little girl then, so I didn't remember those moments at all.

I saw him cry on one other occasion. He wasn't uncomfortable crying in front of Marisa, so my best guess is he didn't want to appear weak in front of his children. On that occasion, I caught him off guard. He didn't know I was coming home early. It was right after Marisa disappeared. I think he realized then how much he truly loved her.

We'll try to talk some sense into her this Christmas. Everything will be all right, my love, you'll see.

When our aunt and her daughters arrived in a cab from the station, I looked closely at the woman, who very much resembled our grandmother. Of my father's mother I had only seen pictures, because I was almost a baby when she passed away, and also because she had lived in an institution for a long time before she died.

Another thing my parents had lied about.

We were led to believe that our grandmother died peacefully in her bed surrounded by loved ones on a bright day and went straight to heaven with the baby Jesus. That's what they said when we started asking questions. When we realized we only had one set of grandparents instead of two. I only came to know the truth about how she died alone in a hospital bed because one of the neighbors in town mentioned it in passing to Marisa when talking about another elderly woman who was also a neighbor.

Marisa had taken us shopping with her and we stumbled upon this old parrot by chance.

"It is very sad that she ended up like this, alone and sick in the head, like Guillermo's mother," said the woman, squeezing Marisa's arm tightly.

All the blood drained from our mother's face. I knew immediately the woman said something she shouldn't have. Marisa tried to act normal in hopes that we hadn't caught it. Carlos didn't. His attention was always where it shouldn't be, never where it was needed. But I was curious enough to ask Marisa afterwards. She had to struggle with the words to make the whole thing understandable to a nine-year-old.

"She had ... some issues, your grandmother. She saw things that didn't exist. Or at least she said so. She did weird, dangerous things, you know? She ended up hurting herself. She needed care neither your father nor Aunt Olvido could provide. They had to find a place for her. They took good care of her there, despite what Anadita said before. Your grandma was the sweetest lady, she loved me like a daughter? Until she got sick," Marisa explained. "You look a lot like her. Aunt Olvido is also her spitting image."

Not that I needed to be reminded of what I looked like, but it did awaken a doubt in me. Had I inherited more than the family's ungraceful appearance? Did I see things in the forest no one else could see? Was my grandmother a witch? A sorceress? Would I end up in an institution like her if I ever dared to share the true story of my dog's birth? If I told my parents or my brother about the Reyes Magos and the oak tree? The heart that beat inside its bark? I was terrified for days, until I realized I simply had to keep my mouth shut. I wouldn't talk about my secrets. Not to anyone. They would be mine and mine alone. Not even as a teenager did I ever tell them to Raúl.

Olvido's girls were as sweet as jam and very innocent. I hope they are well; it's been years since I last saw them. It was not a pleasant encounter, to be honest. A courtroom is not a welcoming place. And even if it were, they blame me for their mother's death. Hopefully they have found the magic that runs under their skin. I don't think the family legacy has turned its back on them. Of course, without the knowledge of how to tap into it, it doesn't matter. Actually, we were never that close. We barely saw each other during the school year because they lived in town a couple of hours away. At most we spent a week together on vacation.

That Christmas Eve the adults were very busy preparing dinner and not at all interested in us children running around the house while there were pots on the fire, oil boiling. Not so much because we could get hurt, but because we could throw or spoil something. Food was the religion of the family.

We were ordered to go out into the street despite the cold. Our village was small and quiet, nothing more dangerous could happen to us than peeling our knees or breaking an arm. Besides, Marisa and Guillermo's way of raising children was the same for their kids as for the *pitos de caleya*. Being outside and not bothering adults was the best thing we could do. Roaming around free was supposed to make us happy healthy children.

I went out to play with Carlos and our cousins against my will. It was going to be Señor Magia's first birthday and there was a lot to prepare before Epiphany. I was going to bake him some homemade sweets I had seen on the Internet under Guillermo's supervision.

In reality, he did not supervise anything, nor did he look at my screen. His *supervision* consisted of staying in the same room as us. Looking at his own computer. I know now he wouldn't have noticed any inappropriate behavior online, because he was busy with his own. Watching us was more of an excuse than an obligation.

Besides, I had not yet decided what to ask the Reyes Magos for that year. I had everything I needed with Señor Magia's company. And, honestly, dolls and games didn't interest me anymore. Plastic and waste.

All I wanted that Christmas was to get some answers from my aunt.

I was so intrigued by Aunt Olvido. Staying to listen to the elders talk was my idea of a perfect Christmas Eve evening.

Carlos, on the other hand, was anxious to get away from the adults. He hurried his pace and grabbed my arm to make me go faster. Mimi fell asleep on a cushion on the fridge, enjoying the warmth of the kitchen and the delicious smell of the pots and pans. Señor Magia, as always, followed us to the park wagging his tail and drooling.

We were alone in the park in the square, because it was too cold and all the other children in the village were playing indoors, glued to wood stoves or fireplaces.

"Los Reyes are our parents," Carlos vomited almost breathlessly as soon as we set foot next to the swings. It came out of his mouth like boiling water. "But your parents are getting divorced now, so you may never get presents again, you know, because your mother is *broken* now," he concluded.

Apparently, according to the conversation, he had picked up this information in the schoolyard. A classmate took it upon himself to spread it before Christmas vacation began and Carlos was eager to share it with children who still believed in magic. So far, he had spread his lies with his karate classmates and everyone in catechism class. If I had known about it earlier, I wouldn't have let it get this far.

I was the guardian of magic. My heart dropped to the floor. How dare he? Why the hell did he corrupt those girls with dirty lies? And why hadn't he trusted me before? I could have cured him of his ignorance. Shared my knowledge. Maybe we could have traded the nasty cat for another puppy.

Now I know they were not lies. That it is normal. Everyone has stories like that. But for me, that's the moment I realized our paths had grown so far apart they were irretrievable. We would never go back to being the kids who slept in the same bed, hugging each other tightly trying to catch a glimpse of the Reyes Magos in the kitchen.

Marta and Margarita looked at him with teary eyes, their mouths open in surprise and disbelief turning to tears.

"No, but ... they said they still love us and now we'll have two birthdays, and two Christmases and two houses. Like they said it would be twice as much fun now." Margarita, the oldest, hugged Marta.

I looked at them and realized they believed those disgusting lies. They were eating them as if they were eucalyptus candies. The fools! Sure, lies are sweet, but you have to resist them.

Carlos had just positioned himself on the side of the adults. Working hand in hand with the exterminators of magic. There was no middle ground in that war. Either you were on the side of magic, or you were its mortal enemy. At nine years old, mortal enemies are very important.

"Don't listen to him. He's a liar!" I shouted at the top of my lungs, pushing my brother away from them.

The girls laughed, relieved at the prospect of receiving twice as many gifts. Twice as much love. They were just babies who loved their parents and toys.

"Liar, liar, liar, liar!" they chanted, running in circles around Carlos, who passed between them, his cheeks reddened with anger and punched me in the stomach making me lose my balance and fall to the ground.

When I looked at him surprised and terrified, he threw a punch straight to my jaw that hurt me like nothing had ever hurt me before. Because it wasn't physical pain. It was betrayal. Orange, cold, vanilla-scented betrayal. The final breaking of our trust. That thread was getting too tight and gave way.

We had many sibling fights, but he never really hit me. Until now it had all been pretend. Hard enough to put a period to any absurd argument, but not hard enough to hurt. Neither body nor pride. This was a different punch. A grown-up punch. Serious. Full of anger.

I stood up and tried to defend myself, but he was already bigger and stronger than me. Besides, he was used to playing rough with the other boys in the village and school. I remember he used to say he wanted to make a living as a WWF wrestler.

He would always draw himself with one of those huge, golden belts. With tights and spandex suspenders.

He held my arm behind my back. It burned. It hurt. A lot. I screamed for help, not a cry directed at anyone in particular, just a plea for mercy. But Señor Magia, sleeping on the ground a few feet away from us, reacted with rage. He was there to protect his mistress. His mission in life. He was created from death, mud and magic to serve that purpose. A deep growl came out of his mouth so menacing Carlos immediately released me.

"Back off, Señor Magia!" I shouted in fright at the dog running towards my brother.

Carlos barely had time to get on one of the park's slides before Señor Magia caught up with him.

"Stop it! Stop it! Leave him alone! He wasn't hurting me!" I kept screaming, tears running down my cheeks. I couldn't believe that a being so sweet, so good, could be so threatening at the same time. He became a beast that could have killed my brother. He was bloodthirsty, he would have ripped Carlos' throat open without hesitation.

Carlos avoided being bitten for a few seconds. Señor Magia tried to climb up the steps of the slide, throwing bites into the air. Jaws filled with a white foam, eyes fixed desperately on his target. I seized his tail and pulled as hard as I could. It worked. He must have sensed my pain, my fear passing through my hands to him, because he forgot about Carlos, turned around and licked the tears from my face.

Just like that.

As if nothing had happened. As if he hadn't been a hellhound just a second before.

Marta and Margarita cowered on the ground crying. I fell to my knees hugging the dog, my heart racing. Carlos hesitated before getting down, but it was obvious that the dog's madness had dissipated, and he had resumed his usual state of invisibility.

We exchanged horrified glances. The bristling hair, the snarls, the sharp teeth at the ready. That image would never fade from our minds. I sent Señor Magia home with a firm order and we tried to calm our cousins.

"We want Mommy!" they shouted in unison as if rehearsed.

"It's okay. It was just a joke. We wanted to scare you," I winked at Carlos to get him to play along.

"Yeah, yeah, see? Señor Magia didn't bite me or anything. It was a game," he said, turning around so the girls could see he was unharmed.

"We're so sorry, okay? It wasn't as much fun as we thought it would be." I took them by the hand and smiled tenderly. Like someone who doesn't know how to smile but has read the basic instructions. Retract the cheek muscles. Show my teeth. I must have been very convincing, because Marta and Margarita wiped their tears. They got up and started chasing each other around the park as if nothing had happened. One of them was playing Carlos-scared and the other was playing bad-dog. We looked at each other relieved, but we were still shaking.

"Primas!" I called. "You must promise not to say anything to mother or our parents about the prank."

"The Reyes Magos are not going to give us anything for being naughty if you do it." Carlos joined the conversation. "I lied, okay, I lied. The Reyes Magos do exist. They really do."

The girls looked terrified again and nodded. We all stood in a circle.

"We won't tell. Nothing. Never. To no one."

We spit on the ground to seal the deal.

We knew our parents would take Señor Magia to the pound or even put him down if they found out about the near-attack, and he was not to blame for our fight.

I never knew if Carlos had felt the same significant change between us. If he also noticed this sudden anger towards me was different and would change things forever. We never spoke of this incident again. Marta and Margarita kept their promise when we got home, and so did we. I hadn't thought about it in years. It's funny how memory works, don't you think?

That same night, after the fight, one of my baby teeth started to move. I couldn't be sure if it was because of my brother's blow or simply because it was time to finally fall out. It didn't matter. It was an opportunity to experiment with magic again. Maybe the Magos weren't the only ones connected to my forest. It had not yet occurred to me to experiment without excuses.

I played around the old oak tree, I appreciated how alive it was, how different from the other trees, but I was just a little girl who still believed in fairy tales. Maybe it was a gateway for all the magical creatures and gift bearers to reach me. It was a theory I had to test.

My plan was to hand the tooth directly to the Ratoncito Pérez, just as I had done with the hamster. No more hiding coins under the pillow.

That night I left the house without considering the risk involved. The adults had drunk and eaten so much I was sure they would be exhausted when they went to bed. As I walked, I pushed the tooth with my tongue. Its movement produced a strange tingling in the back of my spine. It was neither pleasant nor painful, but a mixture of both. A sensation one could not resist seeking but could not endure for long. The coppery taste of the blood seeping from my gums filled my mouth.

I went under the forest fence with Señor Magia and sat down in the same place where I buried the hamster. Under my old oak tree. My door. My protector. I leaned against the trunk. It wasn't a rough, hard, cold surface. It was soft, cozy, warm as if filled with pulsing blood instead of cold, sticky sap. More flesh than wood. An enormous power pulsed underneath. I could breathe it in. As I closed my eyes, the branches stretched out to cover my whole body in a tender embrace. It didn't occur to me it could be anything other than a feeling of love. Pain and pleasure, love and hate, all sprouting from the same stem, are but different shades of red in a rose garden.

Pushing the tooth with my tongue was not enough to get rid of it. Determined to complete my little ritual before someone got up and noticed my absence, I swallowed my fear of pain and grabbed the tooth between my thumb and forefinger. It was small and warm. I wiggled it back and forth, back and forth, feeling twinges of pain in my mouth each time the nerves were dislodged. Rattles jingled in my belly. I grabbed a handful of soil with my free hand, pressing hard trying not to make any noise. When the last fibers came loose, blood trickled down my lips and fingers. An intense sensation of pain and pleasure released in my belly like a bud blooming. A tension bursting free. A contraction bursting similar to an orgasm as I would discover years later. I spat on the ground, choking on the blood gushing from my gum and the torrent of saliva that accompanied it. The earth welcomed my blood voraciously. Señor Magia sniffed and licked the ground where I spat. He licked my stained fingers. A swirl of tingles bristled the skin on my back as I felt his hot wet tongue on my fingers.

I contemplated the tooth in the palm of my hand. It was a little piece of me that no longer belonged. The last little piece that would fall away on its own. That would escape to rot rather than remain a part of me.

The wind whistled through branches laden with green leaves in the middle of December. The old oak sang for me without mouth or vocal cords. A requiem for my childhood. I wished I could turn that hollow yellowish piece into a jewel to wear around my neck forever. A way to preserve that sense of change, of growth, of blossoming, of pleasure, of intimacy with myself. So, I pulled out a notepad and pencil I had tucked in my pajamas for this purpose and wrote down my new desire. Then I knelt down and buried it along with the tooth. I addressed it very elegantly to Señor Ratón Pérez.

I ran home followed by Señor Magia. Full of life. Adrenaline pumped in my veins. A small dot of red light at the back door followed by a cloud of smoke startled me. I came to a screeching halt.

Aunt Olvido leaned against the wall of the porch, head cocked with curiosity. She wasn't angry. Rather, she resembled someone contemplating a strange occurrence that for some unknown reason pleased her.

"Tita, I ..." I tried to quickly make up a lie, careful not to raise my voice and wake the rest of the family. Suffering my aunt's anger was one thing, but my parents' would be quite another.

"I didn't ask you anything," said Olvido quietly, inspecting the mud on my hands and boots. "I guess the dog is keeping you safe back there?"

"Yes," I hastened to confirm as I stroked Señor Magia's head, "And you can't imagine how fierce he can be. It's very scary, no one would come near me. I found him there, in the forest."

Would she be more understanding if I shared my secret with her? Would she talk to me more about my grandmother? I noticed the words playing on the tip of my tongue without daring to jump out.

"That's what I was told. Good. Come here," she said, putting out her cigarette in one of Marisa's pots of roses. "Wipe your hands."

I approached my aunt with small steps, rubbing my dirty palms on my pajamas. Olvido took my hands between hers and looked at my palms deeply, very carefully. She caressed lines on them. The soft brush of her nails against my skin sent a tingle down my spine.

"Interesting. The dry oak trees, young lady? Is that the place you call your forest?" she asked without looking at my face.

"Yes. They are my friends. And the trees are not dry, not at all. The animals are my friends, too," I confessed when she released my hands and stared at me.

I wanted to tell her everything as much as I wanted to run to my room and hide in the closet. She took a white handkerchief out of her pocket, dipped it in her own saliva and wiped my blood-stained face. I examined her features as she did so. She did not possess Marisa's obvious beauty, but she was undeniably attractive. There were nuances in the round lines of her cheeks and the straight lines of her nose that composed an intricate puzzle one could not help but look and look and look and look. She was subtle where my mother was obvious, mysterious where Marisa looked like an open book. Her black hair, long and dark, covered her like a protective robe. I remember it well, because it was the first time I didn't mind looking like my father's family.

"All right. Don't worry, I won't tell your parents, as long as you promise to be careful and never go alone without the dog."

"I promise. As if he'd ever leave me," I laughed and hugged Señor Magia.

She probably thought I was playing like any other child, and so she thought Señor Magia was big enough to defend me from any human enemy. Who would take a chance on a dog that size?

"And you don't tell them that I was smoking. Your mother would freak out and give me one of her little looks," said Olvido as she picked up the cigarette butt from the pot.

I nodded and ran up the stairs. I threw myself on the bed with my heart about to explode and the biggest dented smile on my face.

The next day, I ran downstairs with Señor Magia very early in the morning and my aunt was already in the kitchen. Didn't that woman sleep? I doubt she could stay in bed for more than a couple of hours those days, in the midst of her nasty divorce. She walked around the kitchen with a pendant dangling from her outstretched hand as if looking for water. The necklace pointed tautly at me. Olvido dropped it on the floor when she saw me.

"What is that, Tita?" I asked, approaching as she quickly picked up the pendant and hid it in the pocket of her denim dungarees.

"Oh, nothing, baby, just a game. Remember, we keep our secrets. You're up early. Want some milk?"

Now I know that pendulum was pointing to Señor Magia. Neither of us realized it. And I will regret not having trusted her with that secret sooner for the rest of my life.

We sat quietly in the kitchen. I let a few pieces of bread and ham fall to the floor, where Señor Magia ate them while grunting at Mimi, who waited for some leftovers on the counter. My aunt's big eyes scrutinized me. But Olvido said nothing. I didn't say anything either. When I finished the hot cocoa and the sandwich, I asked permission to go play.

"What would your parents say if they were awake? The darkness won't cover you now, and I don't want either of us to get into trouble."

"They would say yes. I did all my chores yesterday, so I earned it," I replied confidently. Being a good girl had its advantages.

"Okay, go then. Come back for Christmas breakfast." She kissed me on the forehead. Although it looked more like she was sniffing me. "Always take the dog, baby. It's a wild world out there."

I guess she was referring to *bad men*, but the comment gave me the creeps. I ran into the woods. The blue morning light streamed through the branches marking the spot. I unearthed from the damp ground an ivory brooch with an oval piece of red coral and a germinated seed in the center. The wind hissed through the branches. I hugged the old oak and a pang of love shot through my sternum. I could have sworn hands grabbed my back. But then she still had no body to hug with. I had not yet given her enough love.

Enough blood.

"Isn't that too much of a coincidence?" asked my father, staring at the jewel in disbelief, while Marisa couldn't hide her concern that I had swallowed my tooth during the night. She grabbed my chin with her hand and forced me to open my mouth to look for the missing tooth. Her touch was like sandpaper on my face. It scraped me.

Guillermo gave the brooch to Olvido whose face contorted in a grimace of disgust when the jewel touched her hand. As if instead of a jewelry piece, my father had placed a dead mouse in her open palm. Marta and Margarita approached their mother.

"Can we take it?"

"Can we?" they asked at the same time.

"No, little ones. It's Coral's. You are too small and this is too precious," she replied, returning it to its owner. "Isn't that right, Coral?"

"It is. It must have been a gift from the Ratoncito Pérez," I muttered with a smile, swinging it in the air for the girls to see, but holding it firmly. I wondered why she wouldn't want the girls to touch it.

"Yeah, sure, come on. Or it could be the work of a little thief, since magic, well, you know, it doesn't exist," answered Carlos, eating a cupcake.

"Carlos," Marisa scolded as the girls laughed.

I sneered at him. Hadn't we resolved that issue the day before? I held in my hands the proof magic was real. Again. I hated him with all my might. My guts burned as if I had swallowed red-hot coals. I wished I could ask the Reyes Magos for a different brother. And I felt it with all my heart.

ESTELA

I t can't be.

I get up, leaving Coral's frozen haunting smile on the laptop, and go to the bedroom, my heart pounding against my ribs like a wrecking ball. I open the jewelry box on the dresser in the bedroom.

It is impossible.

No.

I must be going crazy. It's just a coincidence.

I take out the red brooch Eva gave me the day celebrated our anniversary in April, shortly before the insemination. An oval piece of red coral with a germinated seed in the center, as if trapped in amber.

"What have you done to yourself, amor?" I asked her when she came home, before the appointment. Her hand was bandaged.

"Nothing, honey, yesterday I cut myself during breakfast at the hostel. Antonia gave me a half-broken cup and when I went to pour my second coffee it broke in my hand."

I removed the bandage and kissed the cuts across her palm. I didn't give it another thought. We went to dinner, drank, danced and then we made love like those first months after we met, when our bodies were unexplored territory willing to be discovered. Conquered.

"I'm sure it will work this time. That's why I ordered this brooch. A seed growing between us."

I loved her so much that night, naked and sweaty in bed, with her head resting on my belly and her hands caressing the jewel resting between my breasts. I was overflowing with so much happiness it was easy to ignore my own misgivings about the baby. Not to listen to that voice that whispered, and whispers, I will be a horrible mother, that I will always regret it. It is possible those voices will dissipate the moment I hold her in my arms.

That's what everyone says.

But it was easier to cope with this oppressive feeling when Eva was alive.

How can I even be thinking these things.

CLR_INTERVIEW_DAY FOUR.mp4

EVA: I brought you something. Do you know that last week, before I left, we talked about what you missed the most?

CORAL: Oh, no, you haven't. Yes?

EVA: Yes, yes, here. A box of *casadielles*. My mother-in-law makes them even better, but this weekend I had an argument with my partner when I got back. And it didn't seem right to ask her for some *casadielles* so I could keep pissing off her daughter by coming here.

CORAL: [laughs] I guess not. Thank you. Oh, these are ... delicious. Thank you. Would you like one?

EVA: Sure. Shall we start?

CORAL: Hmm.

EVA: At some point you had to know what your brother was saying about the Reyes Magos was the truth. When did that happen and how did it affect you?

CORAL: It was after our tenth birthday when I began to suspect magic didn't come from the Reyes Magos, the Ratóncito Pérez or the Easter Bunny. As childhood faded, so did folk tales, myths, even faith.
All the other children had accepted the simple fact that gifts came from their parents, and I had no choice but to give in.
However, it didn't bother me. The magic of my forest was far more fascinating than three old men handing out gifts to children pretending to be good. It was as if the adults were bullying children into doing things they didn't want to "or else." However, it still felt like a betrayal to me. A totally different and worse one. Marisa and Guillermo had tried to manipulate us.

And it worked.

We were weak.

CORAL

I never went back to the old neighbor's house to read her magazines aloud. I stopped helping Carlos with his homework, and he began to fail. If I kept doing mine and behaving at school it was because I was sure going to university in Madrid was my best chance to get away from the family I despised and the village that was too small and boring for me. The same village I would die to be in right now. What I wouldn't give to wake up in the absolute silence of my childhood bedroom. The cold coming in from the river. The farm animals stirring.

Alone in the forest, playing with Señor Magia, I found peace and happiness those days. The oak tree sang me new lullabies, spoke to me in a language I could understand but could not put in real words. I wish I could explain it better so you can get an idea of the connection I felt with that piece of land forgotten by adults. The oak tree cheered me up on sad or lonely days. It would congratulate me with rays of sunshine that shone like stars through the leaves when I got good grades. It laughed at my jokes through birdsong. It played with me and Señor Magia through lizards and mice.

But it also taught me things. Asked things from me. One morning, before school, the branches of the oak tree were unusually low. Its leaves looked like delicious candy. I had never wanted to eat anything so much. I was not repulsed by the black, winged insects that had landed on them. Nor the thick veins that ran through them. I plucked one that came loose as if it were willingly sacrificing itself. I placed it on my tongue, as I had seen the priest do during communion in church on Sundays. I closed my mouth with the fear and excitement that accompany first times, and began to chew, slowly, as if afraid of hurting the tree by crushing its leaves with my teeth. The initial ochre taste soon became sweeter than honey. With each bite I became just another part of the forest. A piece of a complicated clockwork mechanism, a single body and at the same time a multitude of disordered limbs. I took off my clothes as if they were a skin I no longer needed. The wind caressed me. Birds nested in my rib cage. Ants crawled up my legs. My feet grew like roots looking for water. I could distinguish in my blood turned into sap the different flavors of the earth beneath me. The sun giving me life. The tender shoots of new branches coming out of my navel. I closed my eyes and felt for the first time her presence. It was not just a tree. Where I had been covered by bark, the tree had grown skin. Even though I couldn't see her, I knew she was there. Bubbling all around me. A body melting into mine. The old oak kissing me tenderly on the mouth. Tongues, branches intertwined. Saliva and dew. Magic was something sacred and private, something that belonged to me and no one else. Intimate. Forbidden and wrong, but nothing felt so right. Blood and sap ran equal parts through my veins.

That was the first of many. Like an addiction difficult to control. Once the oak was inside me, there was no turning back.

The other kids in town were only interested in dolls and soccer. I lost all my friends. Not only did I not want to spend time with them. My behavior was rude enough that the other parents didn't want me around their children. The look in my eyes unnerved them. The tone of my voice. I acted like I was raised to be a queen, a goddess among vermin that made them feel judged, but overall, small. I don't blame them.

Marisa and Guillermo were worried, but, somehow, I convinced them that everything would get back to normal sooner or later, that I was just going through a phase, so they left me alone.

When I realized that magic came from the forest and not the trickery of the elders, I spent my afternoons doing little experiments in the forest accompanied by Señor Magia. I knew—I could feel it in my bones—the old oak wanted something from me. It was demanding, it was pressing, almost unbearable, but I had not yet imagined the extent of its desires.

Her desires.

The only thing I was sure of was that I wanted to fulfill its demands. The need to please was already ingrained deep in my soul. Perhaps it had been there from the moment I was born. Maybe it felt it in my useless, impotent half-witch blood.

One night I snuck out of the house before dinner and buried my most beloved doll near the old oak tree. I hadn't played with her since the day I dug up Señor Magia from the hamster's grave. But I still felt a deep connection to her. It was a memory of a simpler time when I trusted my parents and loved my brother. The doll was there the next day. Covered in dirt and lifeless. I didn't bother to take it back home. Whatever I thought I felt for the doll obviously wasn't strong enough, so I threw it in a dumpster on the way back.

On my second attempt, I put a coin that *Güelito* had given me in a piece of old pajamas. It was important to me. My mother's father had died before our eighth birthday, but we had a very special relationship. Very close. That had been his last gift. Once again, the forest didn't seem to care about human sentimentality. I left the coin in the earth in the hope it would somehow find its way back to my grandfather.

Pressing myself against the trunk of the tree, listening carefully to its murmur, its desires, its branches became entangled in my hair. I tried to undo the knots that formed between the leaves to free myself, but the tree was stubborn.

So that's what it wanted.

When I understood, the tension eased, and my hair fell back over my shoulders. I returned the next day with a pair of scissors from the kitchen. I knelt on the roots of the tree and cut off a lock. I buried it right there.

This time the old oak gave me something in return.

From the roots of the tree where I planted my black curls, the sewn hand of a small rag doll was sticking out. I carefully pulled it out of the earth. It had my hair. My features embroidered with dried grasses. It was not soft. It made the crunching sound of leaves on the autumn ground. Dead twigs, moss, dried foliage and stones stuffed her instead of soft cotton. It looked like me, but all twisted and wrong. Its eyes were two uneven stones sewn together with red thread in the shape of a cross. Empty and at the same time fixed on me, scrutinizing me, following me. That lifeless grimace mocked me. The thorns stuck in my fingers when I inadvertently squeezed it too hard. I dropped my doll and became dizzy as she plummeted. I lost my balance and fell to the ground beside her. When I roused, I ran home and hid the doll under the mattress. I tucked it into an old t-shirt and tried to forget it was sleeping under me.

But as I closed my eyes and fell asleep, it hovered over me. My skin was made of patches sewn together with dry leaves and grass. The doll tried to push its way into my belly through my navel. Opening my skin with its thorns right through my new seams, while I was helpless to do anything about it. When the stitches broke, inside me there was no blood, no muscle. I was nothing but sap and moss. Fungus and twigs. Dark, cold mud full of insects. I tried to scream, but my voice was only wind hissing through the trees. I couldn't move, just lay there unable to stop the doll's advance inside me. Searching for my womb to curl up inside. Not even Señor Magia could help me in my sleep.

The next morning, I hid the doll in the corn crib.

I was afraid. What happened made no sense. It was the first and only time I doubted the oak tree. I kept my distance for a couple of days. But when the fear faded, I became convinced the nightmare had been just that. A bad dream. Not a bad omen. Not the manifestation of some evil wish from the forest. Just my mind playing tricks on me because the doll looked awful. Maybe that old magic oak didn't know what human dolls looked like. Maybe that's how the oak tree saw me. Full of leaves and thorns. Powerful. A child to be feared.

I went back to the tree and apologized. But I kept the doll in the granary anyway. It was in the press during the trial. I, too, would be shocked and horrified and draw the wrong conclusions if I saw it for the first time now. No context. But I didn't make it as they said.

My parents had put a bird feeder in the yard years before. The birds liked it, and nests started to appear around the house. Once, I stole a tiny sparrow from a nest, snuck into the woods and broke its neck, sitting under the singing branches of the oak tree. I kissed the sparrow before burying it, because I was sure that this honored a life that had just been taken.

"Sleep well, little bird, you will soon live again," I murmured as I placed handfuls of earth on the little corpse.

The next day, I cut myself deep on the crown of blackberry thorns that appeared where I buried the bird. It was thick and twisted and the thorns were sharper than claws. It enraged it somehow. For the first time in my life, regret flooded me. It was a sticky feeling like snail slime dripping over my mouth. It made my rib cage shrink. My stomach was uneasy. I learned this way, with pain and blood, that my oak tree had its own rules. Rewards and punishments. The whole forest was a place to honor, not to steal lives from.

Death was not what the oak wanted from me. It craved the lives of strangers to feed on. I understand that now. I didn't back then. I still lived by my grandmother's words. No life is wasted. We all come back. Improved. To keep learning.

In spring something changed. Aunt Olvido, after the last failed attempt to save her marriage, moved in with us for good. Although the true nature of the problems that led her to live with us without the girls was never fully revealed by our parents, it was obvious Olvido had not only not taken a step backwards following in her mother's footsteps but had gone further.

Marisa didn't like the new living arrangement. That was clear to anyone with eyes and ears. She was stressed about her sister-in-law and having lost her craft room, but Guillermo seemed happy to help. Totally oblivious to the tension between the two women, or my fascination with my aunt.

When I saw Olvido with a tarot deck on the kitchen table, a couple of days after the move, I was overcome with immense happiness. The secret throbbed in my chest, desperate for light. Desperate to be shared. I'd only ever seen such a deck of cards on our local late night TV shows. But this one didn't strike me as a tease, something to steal money from desperate people.

"Can you read the future with that, Tita?" I asked, sitting down at the table with her.

"It's not exactly that, it's more about understanding," she replied, pressing her cards against his chest. "Do you want to try?"

I nodded eagerly. At last, magic was escaping the forest and entering my home. Someone would answer my questions. Even the ones I didn't dare ask.

"Come on, Olvido, put that away," said Marisa when she entered the room with the tablecloth and some plates.

"Marisa, she was going to read the cards," I complained.

Carlos, who followed our mother carrying glasses, laughed out loud. Earning a look of hatred from myself.

"I'd rather you didn't put any strange ideas into the mind of my young daughter, who already gets carried away so easily, please," Marisa asked, feigning politeness, although her voice sounded as rough as a fork against porcelain.

"I just thought it might be fun to use our imagination a little. Get to know ourselves."

"Coral knows herself well enough." She closed the matter, almost throwing the dishes on the table and leaving in a rage.

I looked at my aunt in amazement. She was fierce. Defiant, yet polite and kind.

After dinner, when I was sure my parents were asleep, I went to my aunt's room. But it was empty. She was downstairs. On the porch, smoking something that didn't smell like teachers' cigarettes, but stronger. Sweeter. I sat down next to her.

"Did you get your period yet?" asked Olvido before I greeted her.

"No," I answered, embarrassed.

I knew some of the girls in my class were already *women*, as they themselves had announced, although I wasn't sure a little blood could be the only ingredient responsible, and Marisa had explained to me the gory details of the process, but I hadn't gone through it yet.

"Okay. We'll do a reading when it's time. I won't disrespect your mother until I have to. She's helping me a lot, you know? I know she doesn't want me here, and we don't want to give her any more reason to kick me out, do we?"

I nodded. I could wait. The prospect of entering the realms of magic with an adult excited me. Someone to really talk to, to ask questions that wouldn't hang in the air and float among the branches unanswered. I wanted to take my aunt into the forest. To share my secrets with her. The urge was already overtaking the desire to keep them to myself. We held hands and stood in silence. A sweet energy overflowed from her and entered me through my skin.

FROM: elisch@modelo.com

TO: evavillar@truepod.com

SUBJECT: Re: Interview Request - Inmate #1814

Dear Eva,

I regret to inform you that your request for an interview with inmate #1814 has been denied. Neither I, nor any other staff member objected to it, but he simply does not wish to participate in the recording.

He seemed open to the possibility of giving a written statement, for which I believe he already has your mailing address.

I'm sorry, and I wish you the best of luck with your podcast.

Sincerely,
Elena Martínez

CORAL

A whole year passed without incident until the morning I woke up with my underwear sticky between my legs. I slipped my fingers inside my panties and retrieved them covered in a chocolate paste with the smell of raw life.

I was not afraid.

I was glad.

I wasn't even afflicted with the pain my peers talked about when they shared their experiences with their periods. All my brain could think was the time has come. I ran to the bathroom, cleaned myself up and snuck into Aunt Olvido's room with my dirty underwear in one hand. Displaying it as if it were a trophy, a flag to announce me free of Marisa's laws.

"Tita ..."

She was the only adult in the house I referred to with an affectionate nickname, much to my mother's horror. Olvido opened her eyes, stunned. When her eyes focused on, she smiled and opened the blankets for me to slip inside. I sank my head into my aunt's chest and inhaled her scent of clean linen and cinnamon.

"We'll do a reading tonight," she said, kissing me softly on the mouth. It was a sweet gesture that deepened the intimacy between us. I was now part of her coven.

"Can we do it by the oak trees, please?" I asked in a soft whisper.

"Of course. I can't wait to see your special place. I thought you'd never invite me."

We waited until the night was still, quiet. Everyone had gone to bed. The snoring of the family vibrated the walls of the house. Olvido, Señor Magia and I crept downstairs. I was so excited to have an adult by my side, someone real, someone with lips and tongue, with eyes and hands to hold and not just an old tree with a heart beating under the bark and a pressing demand.

When we reached the fence, Olvido took a step back. As if she had been hit by a powerful wave. Her eyes went wide like twin moons. I should have explained to her earlier what to expect, but I hardly understood it myself. All I knew was that the old oak tree was alive. It had a will. It was powerful and magical, and it wanted something from me. I didn't know if the experiences I had chewing on its leaves were real or hallucinations. I didn't know how any of it worked. Only that I had to share it with her.

"Come on, Tita, this is how she welcomes us." I grabbed her by the sleeve of her dress and forced her into the forest, where the light was golden, the air warm and the magic real.

The oaks sang for us in that language only I understood. I smiled and pointed to her ear, signaling to pay attention but was a little disappointed when the horror on Olvido's face did not dissipate. Fireflies surrounded us as we sat on the grass and Olvido pulled her deck of cards from her purse.

"I don't know if we should ..." She hesitated, "There's something wrong. This place ... it's not right, little one. Can't you feel the evil all around us, tugging at our hearts?"

What did she mean by that? How could she disrespect my oak tree like that?

"No, evil? It's not evil," I whimpered and took my aunt by the hand. I wanted to show her *evil* doesn't feel good. And this was the best feeling in the world.

"Feel," I said, pressing Olvido's hand against the tree trunk.

She closed her eyes and trembled. Barely suppressed a scream, a deep howl, she wanted to pull her hand away from the tree, but the oak would not let her. Merging her flesh with the wood. Engulfing her. Feeding her into itself.

"No! Let me go! Let me go!" she shouted. Her voice was distorted. Full of pain. The oak let go and Olvido lost her balance. She raised her hand speckled with black splinters bursting through the skin, as if instead of sticking through, they were growing out from the inside. Blood dripped onto the damp earth where Señor Magia licked it. The grimace on my aunt's face twisted as the splinters grew. The tarot deck was scattered on the ground. A fresh wind swept and blew the cards away. Like colorful birds they disappeared into the night.

"We have to go," shouted Olvido, angry and frightened, taking off her cardigan and tying it around her bloody hand. "Now, Coral!"

She put her hand around my arm and forced me to stand up.

"We have to go back," I protested, as the woman pushed me out of the forest.

"Silence," said Olvido, sprinting toward the house. Even Señor Magia had to strain to keep up with her. In silence, we went up to my room.

"What did it give you?" she whispered, looking around the room.

"What do you mean?" I asked, pretending.

I was very confused. Everything was wrong.

"The brooch, where is it? And what else?" Olvido opened my jewelry box and retrieved the present the oak tree had given me in exchange for my last milk tooth.

"Nothing."

I was scared and didn't want to mention Señor Magia.

"Just a ... a doll," I confessed as a way of calming my aunt's frantic search. I didn't want my parents to find out about my trips to the forest and Olvido was going to wake them all up.

"Where is it?"

"I hid it in the granary. It was so ugly," I pointed to the *horreo* visible from the window.

"Let's go," said Olvido, pushing me towards the door.

Olvido stood silently in the middle of the granary holding the doll with trembling hands. She was cold and afraid. The night was supposed to be magical. My aunt was supposed to confide in me at last that grandmother and herself were witches and that

I was one too. Everything was going wrong, and I didn't know what to think. My mind raced a mile a minute, but I didn't dare say anything to interrupt my aunt, lest I somehow make it worse. Whatever it was.

"We have to get rid of it. But how?"

"I don't want to get rid of her. She is a magic doll, a witch, fierce and powerful like you and Grandma. I also have magic inside me, the oak tree only helps. I don't know why she did that to you, it was a misunderstanding," I protested in whispers as if I was defending a friend.

"Witch? What–what do you mean? Grandma was not a ... I am not ..." Olvido looked as bewildered as if I was speaking in tongues.

"You are! Mom told me that she could see things, hear things, just like me, and that you taught Marta and Margarita witch-craft, and that you can read the future and ... I can talk to the trees and bring gifts from the earth and–"

"No, nena, no. Yes, your grandmother was well-known in our village because the deceased came to visit her, to give her messages for the living, and I do read people's energy. I can use it to heal them. But I'm afraid you don't have those gifts, nena. Your father didn't get them. Men don't have them and that's why it's impossible for him to have passed them on to you," she answered, perplexed. "If I had known you had those thoughts in your head, I would have made it clear to you long before tonight. I am very sorry for that."

"But the doll? The oak tree?" I protested again.

"That's no oak tree, honey." Olvido clung tightly to my shoulders, digging her nails into my skin. "There's a conscience in there, a soul that beats, and a plan. It's not a friend of yours. It's an evil spirit. Who knows if it's a xana or a demon. It could be anything, but it's dark and dangerous."

"NO!" I shouted freeing myself from my aunt's hands. "You're lying!"

I no longer cared if the rest of the family woke. Rage was building up inside me, like a flaming cauldron about to overflow. Señor Magia started growling and baring his teeth at Aunt Olvido, who got up and walked slowly backwards.

"Coral, hold the dog, please," she begged.

"You are just like Marisa and Guillermo, and all the other adults. You are a liar, and I hope I never see you again," I said quietly, picking up my doll from the floor and I went down from the granary as fast as I could, followed by Señor Magia.

I ran into the house and up to my room. I got under the bed where it was darker, and colder. I grabbed the blankets and pulled them under the bed with me. I turned into a butterfly cocoon. A caterpillar about to dissolve. I cried silently, as adults do. Inside the blankets, holding my wrist, cutting my hands with their thorns I felt safe. Safe from the words I had heard. Safe from the hatred I had felt. I couldn't believe what had happened. Betrayal again. Orange. Cold. Vanilla. Señor Magia's paws were trying to enter my nest, but I wouldn't let them. I wanted to be alone. To dissolve into a tender pupa and forget everything and everyone. Drinking my own tears, I finally fell asleep.

CLR_INTERVIEW_DAY_FIVE.mp4

EVA: *And?*

CORAL: *And* what?

EVA: Well, clearly something else happened that night. According to all the
other accounts, that was the night that
she ... died.

CORAL: Nothing else happened that night,
as far as I know. Nobody heard from
Olvido again. Not even her daughters.
Nor her ex-husband. Since I came out of
the cocoon under my bed I expected an
apology. When I found the letter in my
aunt's room I was really pissed off.

"Sorry, I have to get back."

I ran with Señor Magia into the forest,
but Olvido was not there. I hugged my oak
tree.

"I'm so sorry for the hateful things she
said to you," I whispered, placing my
lips against the trunk. A soft wind blew

through the branches and into my lungs.
It smelled of copper, of bitterness.

Olvido's things were still at home, but
everyone thought her letter meant she
wanted to return to her daughters. It
would have been the most normal thing
to do, since she had not seen them for
a whole year. Guillermo worried she was
suffering from the same illness as her
mother and that she was lost, unable to
find her way home.

The police seemed to be more inclined
to Marisa's theory that Olvido had left
to start a new life elsewhere. Olvido
was of legal age and there was no law
prohibiting adult women from starting
over and forgetting their families.

I had never felt so betrayed. Not even
when I discovered my parents were trying
to pass themselves off as the Reyes
Magos. Nor the first time Carlos hit me.
Not only had Olvido not kept her promise
of a tarot reading, but she had disre-
spected the oak tree, called it evil,
said horrible things about the forest.
She denied me the chance to be part of

the family coven and then abandoned me. If she really believed those vile things she said, why had she abandoned me to my fate? Did she love me so little? Had she ever loved me at all?

I spent whole nights crying myself to sleep. It was only in the embrace of the oak tree that my heart was soothed. How could I not realize she was so close?

So close I should have felt her.

EVA: Do you think you could have suppressed the memories of—?

CORAL: No. And I hope you didn't come here expecting me to suddenly change my story and confess to the murder of Olvido, because I'm not going to lie to make your fucking podcast a success. So. It's the truth or nothing. I'm sorry. I don't remember doing anything to my aunt, because I didn't do it. She did. She knew Olvido would help me out of her spell, and she still needed me.

CORAL

I ate the oak leaves every day. It helped me to cope. Feeling rooted, impassive, great and sacred. It made me forget my stupid aunt and her betrayal. Rage simmered in the bottom of my belly. I despised my mother's opinions about Olvido and me. I couldn't stand my father lying on the couch as if nothing happened, the blue light of the screen coloring the face of a liar who cheated on my mother in her own house. But none as hateful as Carlos.

"I'm glad she's gone, now there's more room for us and more hot water," he had said one morning stuffing himself with biscuits.

Those days we had to go everywhere together because that was our parents' rule. We were not allowed to do anything on our own, but we never exchanged a single word during those walks. Most days we didn't even keep the same pace. Carlos walked couple of meters ahead of me, and I was glad.

Despite being the same age, our friend groups did not intertwine. Basically, I had none and he had many. We were strangers forced to live under the same roof and abide by the same rules.

On the last day of confirmation before Epiphany Eve after Olvido's disappearance, I wore the cream-colored jodhpurs that had become fashionable last term. I wasn't one of the cool girls by any stretch of the imagination, but I was becoming a teenager, and, in my own way, I was trying hard to fit in, as anyone would before realizing it wasn't worth the effort.

Olvido's escape left me with the feeling I was not enough for anyone to truly love me, that I had no friends, not by choice, that I would not have them even if I had not discovered the magic of the oak tree. I still longed for a companion to share my secrets with.

Carlos, on the other hand, was naughty and liked to play at being a bad boy. He and his friends had the dubious honor of being categorized as school bullies. He was a nuisance to both the teachers and our parents, and he made the gap between us grow wider every day.

I had never been the butt of my brother's practical jokes. I thought he still had respect for me. That the pact we made so many years ago with our cousins prevented him from casting his bully's eye my direction. Or maybe he was scared because he could sense my powers, I thought from time to time, holding my disbelief at Olvido's assertion that I was not a witch. Whatever the reason, I was sure he would respect me in public. I even had the impression that, when the time came, he would defend me. I hated him, but it never occurred to me it might be reciprocated.

At church that day, everyone was looking at me. I was so happy. The new pants looked so good. The smile I was showing to everyone still haunts me. It was the smile of a winner, of a butterfly finally emerging from its cocoon for all the world to see. How stupid. Then, the murmur started behind me. Like a flock approaching. I couldn't make out the words, but it was clearly something about me. The fantasy that it could be something good happening didn't last more than a couple of seconds before my brother's voice burst the bubble.

"Oh, fuck. This is disgusting! Hey, guys, look! Is it that time of the month, Carrie?"

I froze. I turned around to look at my pants. They weren't looking at me because they fit. My period had come without warning and, this time, it wasn't a thick chocolate paste that barely soaked my underwear. A wet, red, shiny bloodstain covered the back of my pants and ran down my legs.

"Pig! Go get cleaned up!"

Carlos shouted louder and louder, laughing harder, making everyone look at me. The children echoed his laughter. I didn't know what to do. I had learned my lesson that I couldn't fight him no matter how upset I was. So, despite the urge to hurt him, I decided to run. Carlos came after me.

"We can't go back home alone, you stupid!" he shouted behind my back.

It didn't take him long to reach out and grab me by the arm. I turned and kneed him in the crotch. Carlos doubled over in pain for a second.

"Bitch!"

I ran out again. Blood throbbed in my temples. The red brooch scorched my skin. My cheeks burned. Suddenly, a push and I found myself face down on the ground, with Carlos' weight on my back and his hands holding my head against the mud. Dirty water flooded my nostrils as half my face submerged. I coughed. Panic paralyzed me. Everything hurt and it was hard to breathe with my brother's knees in my ribs. The ground was cold against my burning skin. My belly ached.

"Don't ever hit me again. Don't you ever fucking touch me again. And you better not say anything to Mom and Dad," he whispered in my ear before he punched the ground next to my face. So close my eyes instinctively squeezed shut and mud splattered on me. It trickled down my cheeks. I fell silent.

"Say it!"

"I won't tell Mom and Dad anything," I replied, my words causing bubbles in the murky water that ran into my mouth, choking me.

Carlos lifted me up pulling my backpack and pushed me to walk, ashamed, in front of him. Covered in mud, blood and tears. Humiliated and boiling with rage.

"Amor, what happened?" Marisa ran toward me. I must have looked like I had been hit by a truck.

"She got her period, and some guys decided to mess with her, the assholes," Carlos answered before I could open my mouth. Rage exploded inside, but I held it back. "I rescued her from the mud and chased them away, Mom," he said with a proud look on his face as I kept my head down.

"I'd like to take a shower and pretend this didn't happen, Marisa," I replied. "I know where the pads are."

I wiped the snot with the sleeve of my sweater, nodded, dodged Marisa's efforts to comfort me and went upstairs to the shower followed by Señor Magia, who growled at Carlos every time he moved.

From under the water, as I watched the blood mixed with mud go down the drain, I could hear the faint voices of my parents and my brother. He was embellishing the story to make himself sound even more like a hero. I closed my eyes and imagined my heart turning black and thick, a cauldron of bubbling tar, sticking to his eyes and filling his mouth, his nose, choking him. I abandoned every last drop of love I might have for him in that fantasy of black ooze and death.

I'm not going to deny what I did. I did those things. I just believed too long in my grandmother's words. *No life is wasted.* I woke Carlos up in the middle of the night. Despite our differences, I still knew him well. Like a part of myself. I knew he was weak and his attitude nothing more than a facade that I could easily tear down and use to my own advantage. I don't know if this deep knowledge of him was because we had shared a womb. But it was time to use it.

"I've been a bitch to you lately. Like… the last couple of years? Ever since Olvido moved out and with her gone, it was hard for me, you know? I loved her. But I want us to be brother and sister again. Don't you miss it? I want to forget everything we've done and said and make peace. I'm willing to forget what happened today. I know you have a reputation to uphold. I want to show you something. Make it all up? Please," I whispered, tugging on his arm.

"Hey, I'm sorry about before. I don't know why we do this anymore. I miss it too." he answered half asleep.

"Don't worry, come on. It will be our secret."

Carlos followed me and Señor Magia into the forest.

"Won't Mom and Dad find out we're gone?" he asked hesitantly.

"Oh, no, they never do. I've been doing it since I was eight years old, and I've never been caught once. Only Aunt Olvido saw me come back a couple of Christmases before she moved in."

By my brother's expression, he was seriously impressed by my sneaking skills. But there were also hints of offense, and pity. I never shared those secret night walks with him when we were kids. We were good friends back then. A pang of guilt struck me. Maybe if I hadn't betrayed him by keeping all the magic for myself it wouldn't have come to that. But there was no turning back.

I looked at him, smiling as if nothing had happened. As I would have done when I discovered the magic of the forest if he hadn't been so sure that magic was bullshit. Looking at him, it was clear he was truly sorry, but it was too late. We held hands in the dark. Carlos's palm was sweaty and warm. Soon we reached the old oak tree. I don't know if he saw the forest the same way I did, if the trees were lush and green, or if they were bare and stunted. He didn't say anything, he didn't seem surprised, so I guess we were walking together crossing two different worlds.

"I never told you what happened to the hamster, did I?" I said, letting go of his hand.

"Hamster? What hamster?" Carlos asked incredulously, standing in the middle of the forest. "The one they bought you that escaped on Epiphany?"

"Yes, that one. It was small and gray. It had two dark stripes on top of its back and eyes like two tiny black stones. It smelled like sawdust from the cage. As if it had no scent of its own. It didn't really run away," I replied, circling him like a hungry wolf. I stopped behind my brother. "I traded him for Señor Magia. The oak gave it to me."

Carlos gasped. He was about to laugh. In that situation, even inside the forest, he still had the audacity to try to mock me. He couldn't see the glint of the blade behind him.

I pierced his throat with a knife stolen from the kitchen.

He fell to his knees, coughing up blood, holding his hands to his throat from where a waterfall too thick, too dark was gushing. I walked around him, trying not to get blood on my pajamas. While planning this offering, I half expected to pity him. I even contemplated the possibility my hands would tremble and my heart would soften to the point of confessing everything to my brother. But nothing of the sort happened. I wish I could say otherwise.

As the power of the old oak unfolded around me, my mind was clear, my purpose evident. Seldom have I felt as clear-headed as I did holding that knife and piercing his neck. I sensed the difference between skin and muscle, the hard tendons and bone I grazed. It was something that had to be done and there was no mercy in my heart for him. For that, Carlos would cease to exist to make way for another. I was doing him a favor. He pleaded with his eyes, but nothing could save him from the cold clutch of death. As blood left his body, his face turned white. I pulled a small piece of paper out of my underwear, my wish list stained with the same menstrual blood he had mocked that morning.

I stuck my fingers in Carlos's mouth to open it wide and placed the soaked paper against his tongue. A communion. I closed his mouth smiling. I gently kissed his forehead as his eyes closed.

He fell at my feet like a log. The earth opened and roots of the oak twined around his limbs. The blood on the earth was already indistinguishable from the mud. Señor Magia licked at it, but the stains were not visible on his chocolate-colored snout. The roots pulled Carlos inside of the tree. I knelt next to Señor Magia and dipped my fingers in the blood the earth drank. Then I put them in my mouth.

His blood tasted no different from mine.

I had never given the forest anything that belonged to me so much, so I had no idea what was going to happen. I only knew what I had asked for. Not a different brother, just a better version of Carlos. A brother who was on my side. The exact version of himself he painted for our parents when we returned from confirmation, the version of the story where he wasn't the demon but the hero. Someone who would listen to my secrets. Who would protect me at school. Who would love me as I deserved. A kind, intelligent and sympathetic twin. A brother who recognized my power. That I was a goddess trapped among mortals.

The next morning, my brother woke me up with a gentle kiss on the cheek. There he was, serving breakfast in bed and offering a bag of hot rice in case my ovaries hurt. His nails were broken, bloody and smeared with dirt. His eyes smiled distantly, an expression of serenity more than absence. His hair was plastered to his forehead with sweat and mud. I lifted his chin in search of a scar. Some sign of what happened the night before. But his skin, though dirty, was intact. Virgin.

I was elated to have accomplished such a great task. To have freed my brother from his dark tendencies and brought him into the light with the help of the old oak tree.

My mother's screams interrupted the first truly magical morning between us.

She had just found Mimi dead in the kitchen sink next to the oranges Carlos had cut up for breakfast.

ESTELA

"**Y**ou don't understand."

"No, of course I don't understand," I said to Eva. "I would be relieved if you didn't understand it either before they put your egg inside me."

Coral's account of her twin's murder reminded me of the strongest fight we had. It was before our anniversary, before the brooch and the little girl. That day, I seriously considered leaving Eva forever.

"Coral had no choice, it wasn't her."

"Oh, come on. Wasn't that her? Really, Eva, this whole thing is absurd. You're willing to defend a murderer because she makes you horny?"

"Horny? What the hell are you talking about?"

"As if I didn't know you. But there are lines you shouldn't cross."

We spent hours going over the same thing, shouting the same thing, saying things we would regret the next day. Now that she is gone, has left me for good, I realize I was the one who tried to pull the strings that day. The one who wanted a conflict of such a magnitude it would completely dynamite our plans to be mothers. Our life together. There was still time to turn back. I could still escape that situation. I kept pushing and pushing, throwing everything that came to my mind, nonsense and forgotten stories in her face.

But it didn't work.

At some point, the rope pulling on Eva's heart burst. And a torrent of emotions, of bottled-up pain, of fears, was released like a dam opening the floodgates.

"Estela, I just want this to go well, because ... I need to understand her so that she trusts me. If she tells me where the baby's body is, if I get Raúl Expósito to talk to me, it will be a turning point in my career. I will be free to do other projects, better, better paid ... it won't all depend on you, now there will be three of us and I want to be able to collaborate. I have not been able to carry our baby. I'm not even good for what we women are supposed to be designed for by nature. I'm ... nothing."

She burst into tears.

And it made my heart shrink.

Excerpt from THE GARDEN OF HOR-RORS: A True Crime Company Podcast

Episode 4, aired on June 23, 2018

[Goran Bregovich's Lullaby rises and falls again]

EVA: The most controversial part of the trial concerned this gruesome account of the murder of Carlos López Ramos. Although Coral confessed to murdering him that winter, and the autopsy of the body found in the woods seemed to support her account, multiple witnesses claim the boy was alive for at least two more years, before the day Coral finally snapped and crawled to the Guardia Civil for help. How can we make sense of what the evidence tells us when it is so contradictory?

As I listened to this, looking into her eyes, I believed her. She was very serious and did not try to hide what she did as you may have heard. Why would she refuse to acknowledge any involvement in the murder of her aunt, and then give such a detailed description of how she tricked her brother into the woods to kill him in cold blood? As hard as it is to believe, could there be any truth to her beliefs? Was the oak tree xana real?

Marisa Ramos started a diary after the death of the family cat. It was found by the authorities and used in the trial. Mimi's death was never clarified. It was, according to Marisa, a wild guess by Guillermo that the poor cat had been poisoned by some plants in the garden and had jumped up to the sink to drink water when she started to feel sick, and died there after Carlos left the kitchen. It was not a good explanation. Not for Marisa.

Though, she had many cats when she was younger, she couldn't prove it, and she refused to dwell on it too much, but she knew it hadn't been a natural death. She decided to start a log of her son's behavior. She must have felt so lonely in the house, once her realm of love and soon to be known as the Garden of Horrors. So lonely she could only confide her most unfathomable and bleakest concerns in a notebook, addressed to no one. Let's

listen to my co-host Jennifer read an
excerpt from her journal:

> "No one has helped me dig a
> grave for poor Mimi. No one
> cares. I put her in one of
> those shoeboxes that were hang-
> ing around the pantry full of
> beads and rubber bands. Poor
> thing. I knew it was wrong to
> keep animals as pets. I knew
> we shouldn't take away their
> freedom like that. Why did I
> agree twice? I'm sorry, kitty.
>
> I see the place where I buried
> Mimi from our bedroom window. I
> saw Carlos and the dog playing
> over her remains. It disgusts
> me.
>
> I woke up again covered in sweat
> in the middle of the night.
> Guillermo was there snoring.
> But I had the cat's pleading
> eyes pinned in my head behind
> mine. I swear I heard her call-
> ing for help downstairs and
> that's what woke me. That cat

is always in the sink now. Dying
every morning. Over and over
again. Over and over again I
hear that piercing animal cry
we humans sometimes mimic in the
midst of great pain. The scream
that got stuck in my throat. I
can even hear the snap of Mimi's
neck as the silence becomes
thick in the wee hours of the
morning. Her last heartbeat. Am
I going crazy?"

According to Marisa, Carlos did not shed
a single tear for his beloved cat or
mention her name again. Nor did he seem
to care what was going to be done with
Mimi's lifeless body. Neither did Coral.
She had never liked the cat anyway.

From that morning on, Carlos was a completely different boy, as Marisa noted
in her diary. While it was obvious to
Guillermo the trauma of losing his first
pet had forced his son to reevaluate his
behavior, Marisa could not accept her
husband's explanation.

"Can't you see?" she whispered to Guillermo in bed more than once, but her partner would neither see nor listen. She knew he was happy about the change in Carlos, and also that he was too focused on his latest lover to pay enough attention to the family. But she needed to push him to see.

Apparently, Marisa had known about her husband's blonde mistakes for a long time, but as long as he continued to behave like a partner, she looked the other way. But now, she really needed him to pay attention. To be on her side. She wrote about often. It doesn't sound like Guillermo was too careful. But she never confronted him.

"Now he's happy, can't you see?" Guillermo made fun of his wife every time. It was like trying to convince a wall to move.

Marisa thoroughly interpreted his behavior in the diary. Not having the children fighting constantly and attending to school calls had taken a great weight off the house, leaving Guillermo free to allow himself to be a man outside the home. To be somewhere else where he was not needed but wanted. Marisa could empathize with that need to some extent. If only she had the time and the insouciance to do it herself. But she couldn't.

Marisa's skin crawled every time her son came up to hug or kiss her. I can't imagine what it feels like to despise your own children like that. Even Carlos' smell had changed. Now it was musky. Animal to the point of repulsion.

"He's becoming a man. Did you expect him to smell like a big baby all his life? My mother used to call me *Stinky* when I was a teenager. She said she had to wash my clothes every night so the skunks wouldn't fall in love with me," Guillermo replied in annoyance the afternoon she brought it to his attention. Marisa knew she was going too far. Demanding too much. Needing what he wasn't willing to give. But who else could she ask for help?

Carlos's teachers were pleased with the

good behavior he exhibited at school. While it was true that his grades had not improved at all, at least he was no longer a disruptive presence in the classroom. The teachers told Marisa and Guillermo they should consider what craft their son was going to choose, because his future did not hold academic achievements of any kind. They were happy to help him get through high school, but they should all be satisfied he would go no further.

Guillermo didn't seem to notice what Marisa saw every time the twins were together. Carlos never spoke. He just listened to what Coral had to say. He laughed at her jokes. He kept her secrets. But Marisa never ever saw him trying to tell his own stories. His own secrets. He didn't seem to have any. No secrets. No friends. No will.

According to the autopsy performed by the authorities, he could not have had any. He had been dead for months if one is to believe his bones and not the accounts of those who saw him alive repeatedly for two more years. The other strange thing for Marisa was that Señor Magia couldn't

get enough of Carlos. The teenager and
the dog had a new bond so strong it seemed
they could speak in a secret language
no one else understood, as her daughter
used to do before. It wasn't right. It
was uncanny. Twisted. Her children had
no friends, and they only seemed to love
each other and the dog. She wasn't even
sure they loved her or their father.

Ever since Coral started calling them
Marisa and Guillermo, she had hoped that,
at some point, she would return to her
old self. That once the difficult years
were over, her daughter would love her
again. But that never happened.

One morning, Marisa found her son sleeping in the doghouse in the backyard.
Let's listen to how she described it in
her diary. Jennifer:

        "Carlos was curled up in the
        animal's brown fur. Breathing
        in unison. They both woke up
        and looked at me at the same
        time as if they were parts of
        the same organism. I dared not
        say a word to them. I froze as

if I was doing something wrong. An intruder peeping through the peephole of a closed door. I placed the bowl of canned dog food in front of the kennel door and left almost running. I lacked the courage to look back and see if the dog was eating alone or sharing with Carlos. What's wrong with my son? Oh God, help me."

Little by little, Marisa became more and more afraid of her own son. Carlos spoke so infrequently, she almost forgot what his voice sounded like. She accepted that Coral kept her distance, and now she had lost her other baby too. They had been a part of her. They had moved inside her. Fed from her aching chest that cracked and bled. Endured the pain with a firm body so as not to disturb the peace of the nursing babies. She endured it all. The sleepless nights. The tantrums. Her marriage dissolving into a partnership based on raising those two humans. The complete disappearance of her sex life. Guillermo's mistakes.

She endured it all for these children who were suddenly two strangers. More than strangers. They were, in a way, a threat. A very real threat. Marisa couldn't sleep. Or eat. The house was an oppressive cage. As if everyone was watching her. They were spying on her. They were conspiring against her, even if it was all smiles and rainbows. The intoxicating false happiness was killing her softly. She stopped writing before the children's fifteenth birthday. She was going to confront Carlos directly.

"It's over. Tonight he's going to tell me what's wrong. Guillermo has gone to Madrid for a meeting. Or with one of his bitches, I don't really care anymore. Let him stay with her if he's not going to help me. I'm the mother, damn it, I can shake my son and slap him no matter how big he is. Lock him up if I have to, but this situation has to stop. I need to hear it from his mouth. I need him to confess that he killed Mimi. Then I can get him help.

> And everything will go better.
> It will go better."

We have no record of what happened when Marisa decided to confront her son. Coral refused to offer an explanation. She claimed she was not aware of her mother's murder at the time. She thought she had just left, as she assures that it also happened to Olvido. The only thing we know is that her remains were found in the garden of the house, half buried and that it was impossible to determine what had killed her.

The prosecutor's theory was that Coral had problems with her mother. They had dozens of testimonies to back it up. After a confrontation in which Coral could not get what she wanted from her mother, she decided to poison her during one of Guillermo's business trips so she would have time to bury the body in the yard. The body was there, but other than that, everything else is speculation. Conjecture. Circumstantial evidence.

We'll be back next week with the next
chapter: The *Affair* with the Professor.

CLR_INTERVIEW_DAY_SIX.mp4

EVA: I'm sorry I missed our appointment last week. I had to ... well, I wanted to visit your forest so I could offer my own descriptions, include some photos for the podcast blog. It was interesting.

CORAL: I'm sure she loved having company. Was it spring?

EVA: Spring? What do you mean? Of course, it's spring.

CORAL: Yeah, I guess it's hard to tell now. Did you see her?

EVA: I'm not sure. I wanted to touch the oak, to see if I felt anything. You've said every time that it was soft, like lying on a lover's chest, warm, but in fact it's quite the opposite. The bark is very dry, too hard even for a century-old oak. It almost looked like it was made of broken glass. I cut myself, see?

CORAL: Love is different for each person. Her way of expressing love is also differ-

ent. We don't all need the same things.
I needed sweetness, cotton wool, light.
Maybe you need to remember what pain is.
How would we distinguish pleasure without
it? Now you've bled for her. I bet she's
got a present ready for you. Go back
tonight.

[Cut]

EVA: Coral, let's get back to business,
shall we? I have been following some
interesting leads.

CORAL: Leads to what?

EVA: The whereabouts of Raúl Expósito.

CORAL: Raúl died in my backyard. What was
left of him. I tore out his heart with
my hands.

EVA: But they couldn't find his body.
They dug up the whole garden of your
house, even around Carlos's body in case
you had gotten confused. They didn't find
him or the baby.
  CORAL: They didn't find my dog either.
Are you looking for Señor Magia too,

Eva?

EVA: No, but I'm sure there's an explanation for that. Do you think the theory given at the trial is so unlikely? He got away; he knew the surroundings well. Coral, I know this is very painful for you. I think it's the only moment in the trial when you really lost your composure. Is it okay if we take the opportunity to start talking about Raúl Expósito now?

CORAL: It will never feel right to talk about him for many and varied reasons. But I've agreed to this, and I don't want to let you down now. You're the closest thing I've ever had to a friend. No one has ever listened to me before. I'll be as honest as I can, but keep in mind that my opinion and memories of that time have changed a lot now that I'm an adult. Even though being locked up here for the last ten years has not allowed me to have other relationships, therapy helps to understand that what happened to me was not love. It wasn't healthy. It helps somewhat. At least it does.

EVA: I understand, thank you for doing
this. I'm so sorry you didn't find anyone
to talk to first. I can't imagine going
through it all alone. I know it's hard.
When was the first time you saw him, was
it in high school or in town?

CORAL

Raúl Expósito was the most handsome man I had ever seen in my life. Neither in the flesh nor on television, nor in magazines had I encountered such features. I remember his face as if I had seen it yesterday. His hair was black and curly, neatly unkempt, if you know what I mean. Black eyes framed by thick eyebrows that gave him a firm expression. His jaw was wide and his three-day beard very calculated. I still dream about him, sometimes. First love hit me like a wrecking ball. Like a tornado that turned my soul upside down.

I saw him the first day after summer vacation. The village school could no longer serve us, so we went to the high school in the nearest town. The weather was turning cold and the light golden. The trees colored the world in shades of ochre. Except in my forest, where an eternal green reigned. I was walking from the train station with Carlos and Señor Magia, who was playing with the leaves around us, when I saw a man leaning on one of the columns of the school's porch. He watched all the students coming in with such a big smile, as if his teeth were new and he wanted everyone to see them. He was inspecting the students, trying to decipher their personalities with his eyes. You can't imagine what that intense stare was like. He would take you apart if he wanted to.

I saw some parents approaching and introducing themselves. Even though the other adults were fully engaged in that absurd ritual of first conversations, Raúl kept his eyes glued to the children coming through the door. As we were about to pass him, he couldn't help but notice Señor Magia wagging his tail at the foot of the stairs and curling up to sleep.

"Is that dog going to stay there? Without a leash?" he asked with a curious smile.

"Oh, that? It always does that. It's harmless no matter how big it is," one of the mothers talking to him replied before I had a chance to react. It was our second year in high school, and everyone had already accepted the presence of my dog snoozing on the porch until school was out.

"He, not that," I said angrily to the woman. "Señor Magia always waits for us."

"Good to know," Raúl replied without looking at the woman. His eyes were fixed on me with a wide smile of satisfaction. I wonder if he knew right then and there. If it was obvious to him he could play me. Get anything he wanted from me. When I turned to look at him, those huge black eyes pierced me mercilessly. I blushed and ran inside as if my whole body had been caught in a fire. My skin would be covered in blisters if I stayed a second longer next to that smirk, fermenting under the light of his gaze. I ran into the bathroom, locked myself in, and realized I had been holding my breath. I rolled up my sleeves to make sure I wasn't suffering from third-degree burns.

Love rained down on me like boiling oil.

I was covered in a sweet, sticky sweat. I returned to the classroom and sat, suffocated and confused. That rush of uncontrollable emotions was new to me. A minute later, there he was.

"Good morning, class. I'm Raúl Expósito and I'm going to be your new Literature teacher."

He didn't look like any of my previous teachers. His eyes were deep as coal. On the teacher's days he seemed even taller than he already was. That day he was wearing a three-piece suit as if he had escaped from a time machine. However, he didn't look overdressed or disguised; it just looked good on him.

What the fuck, it fit like a glove.

The next hour passed as if I had been stranded in the middle of the sea, his voice muffled by the waves crashing around me. Enveloping me in a sensation so powerful I barely breathed for the entire lesson and felt dizzy as a drunk for the rest of the day. Faint and confused.

As soon as we got home, I told Señor Magia and Carlos to stay in the yard and ran off into the woods. My dog tried to follow, but Carlos put a hand on his head. They exchanged a complacent look and let me go. I was uncomfortable sharing with them the feelings bubbling up inside me.

I crossed the broken fence alone for the first time since I was eight years old. Breaking the promise I had made to Olvido. She wasn't there anymore, so why should I keep it? I fell to my knees, trying to catch my breath. How could that feeling be so powerful, so immense? I could still see his eyes if I closed mine.

I took some leaves from the lower branches. I chewed them, tasting the bitterness until it became sweet. An acquired taste that grew on me.

As my heart steadied, becoming just another part of the nature around me, as the blood in my veins thickened into sap, adolescent love began to tinge the forest with the soft colors of dusk. Pinks and purples trimmed the green leaves of the oak tree. They colored its trunk. An army of yellow butterflies fluttered around me and in the flapping of their tiny wings, I thought I heard a voice. For the first time, it was not a diffuse sensation, the impression of understanding something without knowing why. No. What came to me were words, clear words. They filled my head with my own voice, but they did not come from me.

"Your love, my sweet child, is nature's strongest impulse."

I was not startled to hear that voice articulating coherent words. The old oak finally found a way to communicate with me in my own language. In my own voice.

I was delighted with my new status. I was no longer a child after having burned under Raúl's gaze of smoldering coals. Something had changed between us, between me and the oak tree, because I had changed. What the spirit trapped under the bark for the past seven years had been waiting for. At last, I had proven that I was going to be useful to it. That everything we had shared, everything we had been through fit into its plan. The pieces it had been placing were settling, taking shape. Olvido had warned me, but I had not been able to see it. I didn't have the distance as I do now. It is easy to see the patterns when we look back on our lives, but it is impossible to do so in the midst of the storm.

The old oak was not only more alive than the rest of the trees in the forest, sustaining them in their eternal spring, it was not only imbued with an ancient magic, it also had a will. It had a plan. And I was only the means to an end.

Should I say *she* had a plan?

It still took some time before she revealed her true self to me, but that was the first time I caught a glimpse of her presence. I had heard about the xanas before. Do you know the legends? It didn't even cross my mind at the time...

Did she feed on my love? I suppose so. I guess that overflowing feeling made her more powerful, more able to communicate. To free herself. The lady of the oak, that xana of the forest, longed to devour my love and knew all that I could offer her.

In the hallways of the school, I learned during that first week that Raúl Expósito was thirty-four years old. He had moved from Barcelona to our small town looking for a return to his roots, to a simpler life away from the hustle and bustle of the city. He was looking for peace, they said.

Of course, I was far from the only one interested in him. As the weeks went by, rumors began to circulate around the school about some mothers who were after him. They weren't very discreet about it, to be fair. So rather than assumptions, the rumors originated from mere observation of the facts. They came to him like moths following a light in the darkest night. Even some female teachers showed interest. They shamelessly competed for his attention. They tried too hard. Some even, like Lorena Bazán, would interrupt class to come in and give him candy, or just to ask him any stupid question unsuitable for the slowest students. They would play dumb to get him to like them and I despised them for it. I vowed never to do it. I was a goddess among mortals, a witch with all the power of the forest in my hands, and he would love me for it.

Raúl lived alone with a cat and was never seen dating in public, which only fueled the interest. Every teacher at school, one way or another, wanted to be the ones to get the attentions of that mysterious man. Either they desired *him* or to be his best friends and cool by proxy. I guess some even ached *to be* him. I tried to convince myself he wasn't playing hard to get, that he simply wasn't interested at all in any of the adults who pursued him. Neither men nor women. My senses told me I still had a chance to be the one.

Raúl Expósito smelled like spring. I wasn't used to men smelling like that. Not cigarettes and sweat. Not stale alcohol like Guillermo did those days. But of linen hanging from a rope on a sunny morning. Freshly cut grass. Cinnamon and coffee.

Vanilla.

I was barely a teenager, still a child in many ways, so nights were spent dreaming of him teaching me the names of the constellations. Naive kisses without a hint of tongue in them. I dreamed of our names engraved on my old trees. I would desecrate them like that if he asked me to. Not the oak, not after hearing the xana's voice. But the rest of the forest? He could have asked me to set fire to it, and I would have smilingly complied. I would have even stayed burning inside if it would have made him look at me again like that first time on the stairs.

My feelings were so strong that there was nothing I would not have done to please him. You see, I hadn't the remotest idea of the things he would ask of me. Just as I had not the remotest idea what the old oak tree would ask of me. During those first few weeks I couldn't see or understand anything that was going on. I could only imagine me and Raúl Expósito holding hands at the movies. Prince Charming dreams that no man alive could ever fulfill. Anyway, he surely could not.

I am not the first and I will not be the only teenager who loses her mind for someone older than her, when you can't compare, you have no experience, everything is new. Every look, every gesture, every discordant heartbeat is like reliving an Epiphany Eve, the feeling before opening the presents. All the possibilities, the magic, the emotion.

It should have stayed there. The first time you get your heart broken. The first time you cry silently in the shower like grown-ups do. The first time you learn that you won't die of love.

One random morning before Christmas he winked at me. I had overslept. Carlos woke me up just in time to wash my face, put on some clothes and run to the train stop. We caught the next train and rushed to school so as not to miss at least the second hour.

Raúl was on hallway duty.

He saw Carlos and me running. He grabbed my arm, to stop me, to make me stop running and calm down. Carlos went on his way and entered the classroom panting. I stood there, as if I had taken root on the hallway tiles, staring at the classroom door. Wishing I could run out and go in. Wishing I could stay suspended in that instant forever, with Raúl's hand around my wrist, and at the same time fall down with a thud. Wishing I knew what to say. What to do.

"Coral, calm down."

He said it in a soft tone, in that raspy, gravelly voice of his, but with a firmness that wrapped itself around my belly. I managed to turn to look at him and nod. And then, as he let go of my wrist slowly, he winked at me with the longest eyelashes I'd ever seen. The blackest eyes.

I made a gesture resembling a smile and headed for the bathroom walking slowly but wanting to run. I imagined his eyes glued to my back. When I looked in the bathroom mirror, I was still sweaty from running and sleep. My cheeks were bright red. My hair, pulled back in a childish bun and my eyes, still puffy. I resembled more of the eight-year-old girl who first wandered into the woods than the woman I was trying to become. I was confused. My heart couldn't beat any faster. I thought I would die right then and there. How could a body as small as mine hold all those feelings inside without my skin cracking? Without my seams splitting open like I had dreamed the doll would do to me?

That same afternoon, I left Carlos and Señor Magia at home and crossed the fence to my oak tree moved by an unknown sensation, which invaded my whole body from the tips of my fingers to the tip of my tongue. I was unable to control my accelerated breathing. Nor the tingling that was born in my chest and spilled between my legs.

I leaned against the trunk of the old oak tree. I took a deep breath with my eyes closed and the branches came down to brush against my chin, lifting it up. I opened my mouth and a handful of leaves slipped inside brushing against my tongue, demanding to be devoured. This time, my feet did not become roots. My hair did not turn into leaves.

Sharp black feathers burst all over my skin. My vision expanded and the bones in my arms crackled to become wings. My lips receded and my teeth mingled with the skin hardening it into the black beak of a raven.

I flapped my new wings and took flight over the village, squawking and gliding, seeing the world from the sky for the first time. Until I landed at Raúl's window. He was reading with a cat on his lap. He played old records and smoked. I recognized the smell of Olvido's cigarettes in the air. I stayed there as long as I could. Until the oak leaves lost their taste in my mouth and I went back to sitting with my back against the trunk.

I miss flying.

CLR_INTERVIEW_DAY_SIX.mp4

EVA: I remember there were long discussions during the trial about your consumption of the leaves. Some doctors said that henbane can be found in the forest, and that you were probably consuming that instead of oak leaves. Tree leaves don't seem to have that kind of effect on the human brain. Not even the laurel leaves that the sibyls were said to have chewed.

CORAL: That was not a regular oak tree. Go tonight. You'll see that the blood you shed was good for something. You will have a gift. Taste its leaves. You will understand everything. It will be easier after you do. We never talk about you, and yet, I know you want something. You want it so badly that it escapes in your breath, in your sweat, it glistens in your eyes. Try the leaves. And you'll see.

EVA: Coral, there's not going to be anything there. I'm not going to feel anything.

CORAL: Bullshit. You weren't so sure before. I noticed it in your voice. It's not that you want to believe me, it's that you *don't* want to believe me. You're trying so hard to deny what you already know. She's still there. My child is still there too. She wants to give you what you want.

EVA: You are wrong. This afternoon I will go back to the forest and I will show you what your doctor has been trying to explain to you for ten years.

CORAL: Okay. Promise me you'll try the leaves.

EVA: I cannot promise you that.

CORAL: Then I cannot continue with these interviews.

EVA: [Sighs] Okay. I promise.

CORAL: We will know if you are lying to us.

EVA: *We* will know?

CORAL: Shall we continue?

EVA: Yes, please.

CORAL: A week later, when I was arriving in the morning, he smiled at me. It wasn't a quick one. It was a long smile with his eyes locked on mine. Castanets pounded my ribs from the inside. My palms were sweating. I would explode if he kept looking at me like that. And he knew it. Of course, he did. No one had ever looked at me like that. Something inside me boiled. I was the one who looked away so I could breathe again.

EVA: Your father didn't notice anything unusual?

CORAL: Guillermo was just part of the furniture in the house those days. He would go to work, come home with some takeout, eat in the kitchen in silence with us, and then sit on the couch with beers until it got dark. His face lacked the bluish glare from his phone screen that had been the norm in my childhood.

I guess cheating on my mother was more fun than starting new relationships. I mean, after all, I'm sure he loved her, but they'd been together for so long. He'd go upstairs without even saying goodnight, and he'd do it all over again from the beginning the next day. I didn't mind at all, really. I promised you I was going to be honest, and there is no other truth in this. As far as I am concerned, his crimes against my grandmother, and Aunt Olvido, were never forgotten or forgiven. He was a traitor to his family's legacy. *My* family's legacy. Although Olvido had tried to deny me the right to be part of it. Guillermo could have accepted it. Help his sister keep her daughters instead of siding with his brother-in-law. So, as far as I was concerned, Guillermo could rot in his own grief.

EVA: Couldn't that estrangement from your family be what tipped the balance towards Raúl?

CORAL: I've thought about it all these years. And yes, my infinite amount of love for Raúl Expósito, maybe it just meant I had no one else to give it to.

I was young and had been deprived of all the women I loved. Of the ability to love them. I loved Carlos and Señor Magia with the same affection I had for my dolls as a child. Like I loved spring mornings and hot baths. Not like any real human feeling. The oak took care of that. It raised me to keep all that love bottled up until I was ready for harvest. Until my belly was ready to bear fruit.

ESTELA

I have seen the interview at least ten times now. The first time I thought it was a reflection. The second time I thought it couldn't be. But the more times I watch it, the more sure I am that it can't possibly be a flaw in the video. I'm not losing my mind either. Of that I have all the certainty in the world, because I have seen it, but I would give anything to erase it from my mind, to be able to ignore it.

Coral talks to Eva with the same calmness as always, with that certain shyness and tenderness my wife used to talk about, which fascinated her. Everything develops normally, until they start talking about the forest. The light becomes warmer. It is a subtle change, perceptible only when you become obsessed and analyze every second carefully.

Coral's dark, sweet, hazel eyes, in front of the camera, become sharp, green, inquisitive. A dark green, an almost imperceptible change. Her fingertips darken, blacken and sharpen, but she seems to notice, so she leans forward, and hides her hands under the table, as if she wants to be closer to Eva to whisper. Her voice sounds wetter. Denser.

It can't be a coincidence.

I don't think Eva realized it at the time. She made no reference to it in the notes she recorded afterwards. There's nothing in the podcast episodes about that, and I'm sure, if she had seen it, she would have jumped up and down like a lioness over that detail. They recorded this interview the day before our anniversary dinner. The day before she gave me the crimson brooch with a germinating seed.

I walk around the house, pacing in front of the kitchen cupboard where my wife's ashes are "grounded" as if she is going to open the door at any moment and offer me an explanation. I need to share my doubts with someone, to hear them out loud. Even though I know I'm going to regret it, I go back to Eva's office and pick up my cell phone.

"Jenni, Eva told you something, I don't know. Maybe she thought that Coral might still be under the influence of the xana or something like that?"

"She didn't say anything like that, no. She wanted us to change the ending to lean a little bit more towards that side of the story, but I also believed the end result would be more rounded, more interesting, than if we simply ended up with the more prosaic version. But if you ask me if Eva really believed all that stuff the answer is no. Please, Estela. You have to give me those cards and stop doing this to yourself. You're starting your third trimester and—"

I hung up on her.

The little girl stirred inside me as I pulled another of the memory cards out of the box.

CORAL

Raúl Expósito called me into his office after lunch one day. My essay on Carmen Laforet's *Nada* was very well written. My goal was to impress him. It seems I had succeeded.

"Did someone help you?" he asked in a serious tone. "Did you copy it from somewhere?"

I blushed with rage, offended by the mere suggestion I had cheated. That those thoughts were too good or too mature to be mine.

"No, I did it by myself," I answered, lowering my eyes, hiding my disappointment.

"Well, I believe you. It's just that your brother's grades aren't very good, and with your mother gone and all I wouldn't blame you if your dad or any other adult in your life had helped you. Or maybe a boyfriend? It must be very hard for you to be the *woman* of the house." His tone was more understanding now. Sweeter. I let my guard down.

A woman.

Not a girl.

Not a young lady.

A woman.

He smiled.

"She left a note ..." I began.

How could I explain I hadn't exactly suffered because of my mother's disappearance. None of the other adults in my life seemed to understand, and I was forced to put on a look of sadness whenever the subject was brought up. I had grown accustomed to being abandoned after Aunt Olvido fled our home. However, I was confident he would understand. He had just called me a *woman*, I could stop acting like a child and behave accordingly.

"My mother, she just needs some time to find herself. She will come back. When she's ready."

"Thinking that is very mature. Not all people would have the maturity to see that their parents are real human beings with complex human behavior," he replied, leaning back in his chair, crossing his arms over his stomach. Examining me in detail. As if he was peeling me, like a soft peach under his fingers.

"Marisa was under too much pressure. With us being twins, with her being so young when she got married. My father made mistakes if you know what I mean? That's understandable," I added, encouraged by the fact that he was talking to me as an equal.

"Wow, you really are a special woman, aren't you?"

And you don't know the half of it, I thought wishing I had the strength to have said it out loud.

"Well, that settles the matter then. You got an A on your essay. Congratulations. I'm looking forward to reading the next one," he said, writing the grade on the paper and handing it to me.

Not only was he immensely attractive, he was also affectionate. I thought so. He cared about me and my feelings. I loved him even more.

That night I dreamed of my oak tree. With my oak tree xana.

It was the first time I saw her, and yet her features were blurred, so much so that the next morning I would not have been able to describe her. I had never imagined a presence for the magic of the forest. Not even when I began to hear her voice clearly. In my dream, from the bark of the tree a naked woman was peeling away, trapped behind the hard trunk. Much more human than I later learned she was. Her skin covered in sticky sap. Her greenish black hair tangled in the branches, turning into leaves. Her mouth half-open, anguished, hungry. It was coming closer to me. She wanted to hug and kiss me. Her hands clung to my skin. She scratched my arms. She pulled me to her and placed one of her legs between mine. Her hard skin against my sex elicited the first real pang of desire in my life. Being near Raúl had not awakened those feelings yet. My body had not yet learned to desire. In my dream, she had swollen lips. The half-closed red eyes of someone who has just cried herself empty. Her sweat-soaked hair sticking out of order on her face. Goose bumps. Tense muscles. A being trapped in the agony of the second before orgasm. Demanding. Capricious. Restless. My breasts swelled as desire concentrated inside. It was no longer a formless sensation spread throughout my cells, infecting my mind, but a fluid that left me. My nipples oozed, soaking through my sports bra. The xana shuddered at the touch of my warm hands on her rough bark-like skin. She rested her head on my elbow. From my nipples gushed a thick, earthy liquid, with the same intense smell of raw life as newborn calves. The creature's nose flaps quivered, and it didn't take a second to bring its eager mouth to the offered breast. The pressure of its teeth on my skin provoked a new twinge of pleasure that joined the torrent gushing out of me. I lowered my eyes to contemplate that being feeding on my desire, and she returned my gaze as she sucked the love for Raúl like the venom of a snake. The xana's hand stretched out to reach my other breast. The earthy liquid slid down her bony fingers like twisted branches that squeezed me anxiously. Until she left me dry. Clean. Desireless.

I woke up panting, covered in a thick sweat like the melted sugar over my grandmother's *torrijas*. My panties were soaked and Señor Magia and Carlos were sitting still on the bed. Piercing me with their eyes.

The next morning, I accompanied Carlos and Señor Magia to the train stop, but when the doors were about to close, I jumped off the train. I had to see for myself if she was real.

"Hello?" I shouted to the wind, leaning against the oak tree with no answer. "I know you're in here," I murmured with my lips brushing the bark.

A caress on my back was the first real contact I had with the xana. A branch brushing against the nape of my neck. I didn't dare turn around. She was there, but she was not at the same time. Like the voice that spoke to me without words. I had not yet given her enough strength. I closed my eyes and pretended I could see her. After all, I could feel her.

"Flesh is love, my sweet girl," her voice whispered to me. A voice that no longer sounded like mine. It was no longer just inside my head. It was sticky, bubbling, like water pouring between stones. "Even if you don't know anything about it."

"But I want to know!"

"Don't open your eyes."

That day, I had my first orgasm lying on her roots.

I kept my eyes closed and let the image of Raúl envelop my senses. His curls. His hands. His black eyes. His raspy voice rising up my navel, down my thighs.

"Let yourself go, my sweet girl."

The roots of the oak tree pinned me to the ground. The branches pushed my underwear aside. The lower branches, covered with new leaves, were reaching into my mouth and into my sex. The sap slid over my nipples. Desire coursed through me like waves breaking inside my head. The image of Raúl pinned against my helpless body. His skin against mine. Griding against me. The pleasure grew and burst, dripping, like a ripe peach squeezed too tightly in his hands.

ESTELA

"**I** found him. Cursed son of a bitch, I found him."

Eva shouted from the kitchen. It had started to get hot. My clothes were already too tight. I was making iced tea, looking sideways at myself in the reflection of the kitchen cabinet glass. My body was filling with curves. I was too engrossed to pay attention to her, but she appeared in the kitchen, laptop in hand. The same laptop covered in stickers of 90's bands and cartoons that I'm using now to check her work.

"I found him," she repeated, eager to share her discovery.

"Excuse me, who did you find?"

"Raúl. I found that pig. He is not dead."

The news snapped me out of my trance. After all, I also knew about the case from listening to her talk to Jennifer. From the beginning, Eva had been convinced if she hadn't been able to find his body or the baby's, it was because he had run away. Among the craziest of her theories was that he had taken the child with him. My wife's romantic soul, always willing to trust in the goodness of people, wanted to believe as much as Coral did that Raúl Expósito was more than just an ordinary pig, one of those that are unfortunately in abundance. I think she wanted to believe it because it made it easier to reconcile with her own past, but she was wrong, of course.

I did believe Coral had killed him, in fact, with what little I knew at the time, I'd say I even wished she had. A textbook *good for her.* I was more inclined to believe in ineffective police work in the search for the body rather than there being a shred of love in that pantomime of a relationship.

"But Coral confessed that she killed him. Him, and the baby. Raúl is dead, even if that story is not the one you want to tell."

"I know, but look," she sat down at the table and pulled out a chair for me, showing me the email she had just received.

I read while Eva stood behind and caressed the back of my neck with her fingertips.

Wow. Looks like I was wrong.

I felt so proud of her as I read that email from one of the police officers who had handled the case. That she hadn't stopped looking, and in the end it had been worth all her effort. It seemed the cop's perspective on the case had changed when his daughters reached Coral's age.

"I told you. You and Jenni. I knew I was right," she kissed my neck, pointing to Raúl's new name on the computer screen.

Eva's eyes were shining as brightly as the day the pregnancy test came back positive. Raúl Expósito was never considered a missing person, but he had managed to ensure no information about his whereabouts and his new name came to light. Of course, that man was a snake charmer who beguiled everyone involved. So Coral was never charged with his murder, not only because there was no body, as the official version stated, but because everyone agreed to protect the scumbag.

"This changes everything. Everything," she murmured, more to herself than me.

"It doesn't change anything, mi vida. I'm really happy for you. I'm sure this will make the podcast much more interesting now, but the truth is, it doesn't change anything she did. She's still a killer. And if I may say so, a fucking nut job."

I know I shouldn't have said that. All the light went out of her eyes when she turned to look at me.

She said nothing.

She closed the lid of the laptop and went back to the office. I did not follow her. I didn't want to have to take it back.

CORAL

Raúl Expósito was a diligent teacher. He was dedicated to his work. He volunteered for all the educational excursions organized by our school and didn't care if it was a visit to a museum or to the chocolate factory.

I had always avoided going on outings that required me to interact with my classmates, but staying alone at school or at home knowing Raúl was on that bus was an absurd notion. It was impossible for me to resist the opportunity to be near him again.

Shortly after the meeting in his office to discuss my work on Nada, we went to visit the mining museum. My interest in the subject was nil. I walked behind the guide and my companions without paying real attention, my eyes fixed on Raúl's back.

Until they said we would go down to the galleries.

The cage that carried the miners to the different levels was not too big. My companions began to descend while the rest of us waited our turn. Raúl, who had been among the lead group, disappeared from my sight. I didn't know where he was until it was my turn.

When the doors closed, I noticed he had walked in right behind me.

He was so close his heat reached my body. I could hear his breathing above my neck. My skin prickled every time a sudden movement of that iron cage caused his hands to brush against me. The air was thick. The dim light of the bulb flickered. We were in a crowded elevator and yet I felt like I was descending into hell alone with him.

Suddenly, Raúl's hand on my back turned me into an immobile lump of coal burning in the fire. His finger slowly drew a heart in my back between my shoulders. My breath caught in my chest. My eyes turned into two stones unable to move like those of my doll of moss and leaves. When he finished the stroke of the heart, the palm of his hand traveled even more slowly, exploring every inch of my back until it fell, barely grazing my behind. His chest pressed against my spine. Not so close that no one noticed, but close enough for me to understand it was a calculated and precise movement. His face then moved closer to mine, and just before the doors of the elevator that had taken us to the center of the black, shorn earth opened, his lips brushed my ear.

If the gates had revealed hell itself when they opened, I would have felt no different. Lost, consumed by the flames, tortured ...

But what a sweet torture that was.

Raúl didn't go near me again all day. He sat in the first seats of the bus with the history teacher, Lorena Bazán. When we arrived at the high school, Señor Magia and Carlos were there waiting for me. The others got into the cars with their parents, and we started our way to the train station.

"Coral!" It was Raúl's voice rushing after us. "Here, you forgot this on the bus."

I approached with my cheeks burning, my stomach shrinking, unable to even smile, let alone speak. Raúl held out the field trip material I had forgotten on the seat. I took it, and nodded, but as I was about to turn around, Raúl grabbed my wrist and pulled my hand towards him.

"And this," he added, without smiling with his lips, but with his eyes, as he placed a piece of shiny coal in the palm of my hand.

I squeezed it unable to react. He winked at me and left.

"Don't forget the test on Monday," he said without turning to look at me.

Had that really happened?

I made it all the way on the train in silence, although I could feel Carlos and Señor Magia's gazes burning into my skin. They wanted to know how the excursion had gone, to live through my enthusiasm, but the words were stuck in my throat like a fish bone.

I left them at the station, kissed them each on the forehead and headed for the woods. I had clenched the piece of polished coal so tightly when I opened my hand I found it covered with my own blood and my palm bruised by the black edges.

I knelt by the roots of the oak tree where I had buried the hamster. My tooth. My brother's first version. I rested my bloodstained hand on the roots and buried the lump of charcoal.

"Make him mine," I whispered, kissing the bark of the tree.

CLR_INTERVIEW_DAY_EIGHT.mp4

CORAL: You did it. I don't even need to ask you. [Reaches out to take Eva's hand and kiss it]

DOCTOR: Coral, come on, don't make me have to end this now.

EVA: Yes, don't worry, it won't happen again, right, Coral?

CORAL: Right. Did you like it? What did they taste like? What did you see?

EVA: Bitter, at first. Like honey candy, later. My skin opened up and filled with black and white feathers. My bones uncrossed, my vision became so precise, so wide ... I could flap my new wings and fly. Just like you said. I was a swallow, and I was sneaking into my own house, only it wasn't my house. It was, and it wasn't. Do you understand? There was a room painted pink and a baby. We don't have a baby yet. She was asleep in the crib. With red hair like Estela's. I was banging on the window trying to get

a better look at her. When she woke up
I saw her eyes, dark like mine. Although
that's not possible. My wife, this week
we will know if she is pregnant, but the
baby, it won't look like both of us. It
will look like me and the donor, but not
her. And this little girl was so pretty.
So pretty ...

CORAL: She can look like both. She can be
the biological daughter of both. She has
taught you that. She, who is a treasure,
can give you everything you desire. And
she does not ask so much in return. Pick
up the leaves, dry them and give them
to your wife. The child will be strong,
brave, fierce.

ESTELA

I slam the laptop shut and run to the bathroom to throw up. My heart is about to explode. I can't breathe as my body tries to expel the contents of my stomach, but I haven't eaten anything today. I haven't had an appetite for weeks. I'm too tired to do anything but rummage through Eva's papers. Watching her interviews with Coral over and over again. Again and again, looking for clues to help me understand. Searching again for those sharp green eyes, for the transformation. And there it is. How is it possible that Jenni didn't see it? That Eva didn't run away?

I choke. My eyes fill up with tears, which spill into my mouth, mixing their salty taste with that of bile. I manage to catch a breath of air and let myself fall on the green tiles of the bathroom. Clutching my belly. The girl stirs. I'm overcome with hysterical crying until I'm empty.

I stand up carefully, look at myself in the mirror. I struggle to recognize myself in these round, flushed cheeks. In the swollen green eyes. I go to the kitchen and take out the infusion jar Eva gave me. My first instinct is to throw it away. Empty its contents, which never seem to run out, and run the faucet so it all washes away. How could she do this to us? How could she believe all the crazy things Coral was saying?

In front of the sink with the open pot in my hand, I feel a kick from the girl. In the space between two heartbeats, I notice how my body stops and my perception changes. As if I had been living with my eyes closed for the last few months and now, finally, I have opened them and can see clearly.

"You're nothing but a spawn of the forest, aren't you?" I speak to the girl while I draw spirals on my belly, and her movements inside me make me believe she understands. "I have never felt you were mine, maybe it is not because I am a bad person. Or incapable of loving you. Maybe it's because you're not mine. Not even human. You're nothing but a tumor. A parasite."

What did you do, Eva?

CLR_INTERVIEW_DAY_EIGHT.mp4

[Five minutes of black image]

EVA: Tell me about the messages. I have to tell you in advance that I have read them. Your recount of them anyway. It's part of the summary of the case, so I am aware of their supposed content. But how did it start?

CORAL: One day, Raúl Expósito stopped me before I went out the front door. Señor Magia and Carlos were already waiting for me. Raúl gave me a piece of paper. He didn't say anything else. He just slipped the paper into my hand and winked at me. When I sat down on the train, and opened the folded paper, my heart almost exploded. It was a phone number. His personal number.

"Hi, it's Coral."

My fingers were trembling as I wrote it

down. As soon as I got home, I sat on the bed to send that message. With my legs bent like a butterfly and my cell phone in the middle. Biting my nails and trying to conjure up a response.

"Hi Coral, how did your history exam go today?"

For a few weeks, the messages were innocent. Naive. Nothing too obvious. Nothing that could get either of us in trouble if someone carelessly read them. School stuff. Raúl would recommend books. Music videos. From time to time, he would make innocent insinuations so easily attributed to jokes that sometimes I didn't even know if he meant it as an innuendo or not. Then one day the "Good morning, beautiful" and "Good night, princess" messages started. I read all his messages to the oak tree as I would have read them to any other friend, had I had one available.

But I guess you're more interested in the *Never Have I Ever* messages.

CORAL

One night, the phone vibrated insistently on the bedside table like a hornet trapped under a plastic cup. Startled, I picked up the alarm clock to check the time. It was a few minutes past three. It could only be a message from Raúl. My new cell phone never rang, the *do not disturb* option was always checked. I didn't like to receive calls from Guillermo, nor from the school. Since, apparently, it had become a habit to call me for my brother's apathetic behavior instead of my father. However, a buzzing sound alerted me to Raúl's messages. The vibration, a purr on the table, or in my pocket, made my spine twist and my belly spasmed like a fish fighting for air.

I had promised myself not to read his messages or respond immediately, I didn't want to be demanding, anxious or too available. I may not have had female friends, but I had read books. I had opinions about the women who swarmed around him and didn't want to be like them. However, doing so was as irresistible as ripping out a scab and airing the wound again.

The bluish light from the cell phone stung my pupils forcing me to instinctively close my eyes. I blinked a couple of times, returned to the home screen and lowered the brightness of the cell phone before opening the conversation.

I was surprised to find a voice message. He had never communicated with me like that before. He also never used his real phone number. That became clear at the trial. We deleted all the messages, so I couldn't prove any of it. I imagine he felt safer that way. After all, he was still my teacher. An army of ants crawled up my back. I put on my headphones so I wouldn't miss the slightest nuance in his voice.

"Would you like to try a game?"

Raúl's voice through the headphones was low. Ragged. Wet. A dozen tongues running down my thighs. I listened to the message five times before answering. I let that voice sink into my flesh, soak into my every cell.

Yes, I wrote.

Immediately, the vibration in my hands brought a new voice message.

"Speak up. I'm sick of reading you. I want to listen to you. No one can hear us now. It's just you and me."

No conversation before had that authoritative tone. I suspect he had been drinking that day. I suppose he had planned to play his part a little more, but alcohol and desire conspired against him. He wanted it all. Me. Whole. Now. Right then and there. He didn't want to wait any longer. His drive was demanding. And it infected his voice. If I had been anything more than a teenager, I would have read it in that tone. He had never used it. I had never heard it. Not even when he was in the role of teacher.

Raúl had given me the impression of a confident, immensely talented and attractive person. Affectionate. Sweet. Vulnerable, at times. Protective, at other times. The kind of man who makes you feel at home when he hugs you. That's what I imagined him to be back then: perfect. Someone you confess all your secrets to. At least, that was the Raúl I had built from the pieces he had given me.

That night, before the darkest pit of hell opened under my feet, alone in my room, I loved him. At least I thought I did. The xana wanted, needed, me to love him with all my being. I was trapped. Did I have any choice? Any real choice? No one can judge me without having tasted a minute of magic. Of teenage love.

As much in love as I was, I was also embarrassed to talk to this new Raúl, who was pushing me further out of my comfort zone. I had only recently recognized my own desire. I wasn't ready to share it with him. It was too private. As much mine as my secret oak tree. Like Señor Magia and Carlos. Like my xana. I was used to keeping my secrets, not sharing them with anyone.

I can't now, I wrote holding my breath. It was as if my throat had been cut, air unable to pass through it long enough to produce a sound.

"Well, I guess it's your decision then. Goodbye, Coral. See you at school," replied the messaging voice. Serious. Disappointed. Unfamiliar.

My heart was racing. The tension in my thighs became unbearable. Uncomfortable. Urgent. This parting was like the caress of the cold edge of a pair of scissors on the back of my neck, grazing my chin. I curled up under the blanket, my head completely covered, reduced to a tender pupa, and pressed the button on the microphone.

"I'm sorry. Let's play," I sighed and tried to swallow saliva, but my mouth was a sponge abandoned to the sun.

"Atta *girl*. I guess you know this game. Never have I ever?" he asked, his soft voice again infesting my brain like termites.

"Yes," I was able to answer with fear and desire clenching my stomach.

"My version is different. You'll see. You will like it."

Never have I ever … stolen alcohol from the supermarket.

Never have I ever … taken a picture of my underwear.

Just a game. The slight variation was fun. I had been good since the day I believed in the Reyes Magos. As far as I was concerned at the time, what I had done nothing wrong in the forest. The blood I shed was merciful and only brought me joy, so how could it be anything other than my best behavior? I had improved them. The hamster. My brother. No, I hadn't *killed* them. It still hurts to say it like that. So what I had done, it wasn't like this nonsense Raúl was asking me to do. Despite the blood on my hands, despite the sap on my thighs, I was pure. Instead, that game seemed like a rite of passage to adulthood.

"Let's turn your *nevers* into firsts," he had said.

I'd worked up a sweat recording the video of the theft of a bottle of black vodka. How stupid is that? I felt more excitement as I slid the bottle into my backpack than I did slitting my brother's throat and licking his blood from my fingers.

I felt uncomfortable in front of my bedroom mirror in my underwear, with the door bolted shut so that neither Carlos nor Guillermo could enter. I took a lot of pictures. I didn't look good in any of them. My hips were too round. My belly was childish compared to the women in the ads. My breasts weren't big and didn't look up to the sky. I had bought women's underwear for the first time for those pictures. Interspersed with the discomfort, there was also excitement. Those nerves that some compare to butterflies in the stomach. The need for him to like me.

"You bought those clothes for me, didn't you? You're so sweet. But you don't need to dress up like an old lady. You're perfect just the way you are. In your normal clothes."

Raúl wanted the little hearts, the little dots, the cartoon characters. I wanted to play at being a woman.

He wanted to play with a girl.

The nights became sweet rewards. There was something comforting in knowing that when we played I was not the master of my actions. Just like giving in to the oak tree's desires. Letting myself go and forgetting I had a will too. I felt like a queen being carried away by the vigor of her king. I would fall asleep licking my wet fingers covered in my thoughts, with Raúl's messages playing on loop.

The next morning, we acted as if nothing had happened, so I didn't know what to expect. We had never seen each other alone. We hadn't kissed. We hadn't talked about what was going on when we were each on one side of the phone. If he didn't write me one day, I assumed it was over. That he'd had enough of playing with me, that he didn't really like me. But then, when the phone rang again, I would forget my doubts and think, *If he really didn't like me, why would he risk his job like that?*

During school hours we were only teacher and student. Complicit glances here and there. Sprinkled on normal days like falling confetti.

All the time I wasn't Raúl's toy, I was the xana's. I murmured standing against her trunk, with my lips glued to her, all the games we had invented. I poured my love on her, and every day her body was more real. Her figure not only in my dreams but shaping the tree.

Not all of his games had to do with our relationship, if you can call what he did to me a relationship. He never asked me to send him anything riskier than those pictures in my underwear. They were the things that any teenager with a *normal* life would have gone through.

Never have I ever … cheated on a test.

Never have I ever … gotten drunk.

Never have I ever … smoked in school.

Everything seemed exciting and innocent. Little rebellions. Experiences that made my world bigger.

INMATE LETTER #1418

DATE: June 4, 2018

Dear Eva,

First of all, I'm sorry I turned down your offer for an interview. I would have loved to chat with you judging by the photos I have seen on the web. But I want to get involved in everything that happened with Coral Lopez now even less than I did then.

I was lucky enough to escape the public eye thanks to the invaluable help of a few good men and I would love to keep it that way.

Fortunately, I had left the country before the bodies were discovered. Can you imagine the *shock* when the police came knocking on my door to check I wasn't pushing daisies? Nightmares still haunt my nights. The memory of that little girl haunts me. It is my torment today just as she was ten years ago.

But I wouldn't leave you hanging without
offering you anything. I have never been
able to resist the requests of a beautiful woman. I am a weak man who has always
been played with.

I want to say clearly, once again, some
things that the cops understood back in
the day and that I hope you understand
as well. I've listened to some of your
podcasts and you seem like a very smart
girl.

Prove it.

I never laid a finger on Coral López; I
never had a relationship with her, and
I certainly never had a child with her.
If I had, don't you think there would be
some proof of the fact? Anything? Don't
be simple and try to use the messages
against me, I'm sure you are much smarter
than the journalists who tried to do
that. That phone could be anyone's. I
wouldn't be surprised, seeing as she was
quite delusional, if she had even sent
them to herself.

That girl was trouble. I wish I could have

helped her more. Her mother was missing, her father was a drunk, and her brother was difficult at best. She was bright, though. Coral could have been a great student.

It's the curse of beautiful women to be, in addition, intelligent. Is it yours too?

When I was teaching her, I realized she was in love with me, but I never made her believe it was reciprocal. I loved Lorena Bazán, and I was very sorry for what happened to her. I have never had relationships with minors. My only crime was trusting the wrong people. It is the same one that brought me here. If you have done your homework like a good girl, you will know that my crimes are not of a sexual nature.

If I were to help you, I would only subject myself to more suffering. I have suffered enough, don't you think? I only wish to serve my time here and return to society as soon as possible.

My only request is this:

Don't tell Coral I'm alive or where to
find me.

Best regards,
R.

CORAL

T hings changed the day Raúl Expósito called me to his office. It was not unusual. It was part of his job.

"I'm glad you got here on time," he said in a voice very much like a teacher's as he closed the door behind me.

I would love to say I remember it with bitterness, and of course I feel all the pain it caused me, but, at the same time, I still feel a pang of desire in my legs mixed with a revolution in my stomach. Raúl was my first love. My only love. It was always like that with him, wasn't it? Part pleasure, part fear, part pain, part guilt. It was never worth it. It was impossible to refuse at the same time. I guess it's no different than any addiction.

I lifted my skirt a little before sitting down at the table across from him. I wanted to feel the coolness of the chair on my thighs. I could tell he noticed, but he didn't say anything. I smiled confidently. I was now a forest goddess.

He got up and sat on the edge of the table looking at me as if there wasn't even air between us.

"So, the situation with the other girls is going better?" he asked.

To my disappointment.

I thought it would be a more personal encounter. The truth is, I never had any problems with the other girls in high school. I kept to myself and they ignored me. But I went along with it anyway.

"Uh ... yeah, it's going better, you know. I don't really mind them that much; my brother would stand up for me if someone tried to step out of line. He's the biggest kid in school after all."

"Yes. And the dog," he said firmly.

"What about the dog?" I asked.

"It's a big dog. *Very* big. The teachers talk. Apparently, it defends you and follows you everywhere."

"He does. He's a good boy," I replied. I could feel the tension building in my thighs, I was no longer comfortable. Why was he acting like an adult and a teacher now?

"Would he defend you from ... me?" The tone of his voice was the one I was familiar with.

"Why would he do that? Are you planning to hurt me?" It was a game again.

"Only when you ask me to."

I blushed. He went to the door, and I heard the sound of the latch behind me, but I didn't turn around. I couldn't. That *click* turned me into a statue of salt. He went back to his desk and knelt beside me.

"Never have I ever kissed a man," he murmured, looking at my lips.

I lost track of time, of my surroundings. I was so close, I breathed his minty breath. The warmth of his skin reached mine as if I felt the sun on my cheeks. I thought I might have a heart attack or throw up.

He kissed me.

It was a sweet kiss. Moist. Slow. Brief, because we couldn't risk getting caught. His tongue caressed mine. His saliva was sweet. I was surprised by the taste. His teeth bit my lower lip gently. He squeezed a little harder than he should for a second before releasing. Magic tinkled in my spine.

"You are different, Coral. You're not like the other girls. You are my Torment," he whispered in my ear. Before getting up and opening the door again.

I regret it now, as I tell it. You see, he threw a bunch of old-fashioned clichés in my face and I loved them. I thought he sensed the magic in me.

"Let me know if they get back to their old ways. We have zero tolerance for bullying at this school," he said, reverting to a formal, louder tone of voice so that anyone passing in the hallway could get an idea of what the meeting was about. "We will deal with it."

"Thank you, Mr. Expósito," I said, hiding my smile. My cheeks red. My underwear bunched with the wetness of a swamp.

I skipped the next class so I could catch the train and run to the xana to tell her all about it. To feed her with my oozing heart.

For the first time, when I arrived at the oak tree, she was there. Leaning against the trunk of the tree. Red hair, naked, perfect round green eyes. All irises. Fingers and nails all one, like claws that grew blacker and blacker until they blended into the night. Moss where there should be hair and mushrooms where there should be breasts. I had never seen anything more captivating, more beautiful.

"Who are you?" I asked, although I knew the answer.

"After eight years you have to ask, my sweet girl?" I recognized her voice instantly. As she spoke, I could see her gray teeth, sharp mountain stones dripping water from the springs.

"You are ... so beautiful. You were not like that in my dreams."

"Humans don't have much imagination, my child."

I was paralyzed, not daring to approach, fascinated and terrified, just as Raúl made me feel.

"What is your name?" I asked to break the silence as she reached around me and smelled my hair.

"Your desire is the most exquisite perfume," she mused before standing in front of me and answering, "I don't have a name that can fit your throat, but you can give me one, my sweet girl."

She leaned forward, caressing my arms with her long black fingers, and kissing me slowly as I had seen her do in my head when I consumed the leaves of the oak tree, or lay naked on its roots. The feel of her tongue was slimy, flooding my whole mouth as if I was trying to breathe underwater. To describe her taste would be impossible. It would be like asking the sky what it feels, what it sees when it looks down to earth. Her kiss was every Epiphany Eve before the betrayal. The games with Señor Magia and Raúl's eyes. My favorite song and the grass under my feet.

"Ayalga," I managed to answer when she broke away from me. "Your name is Ayalga."

After the first kiss, Raúl and I texted each other more often. More and more risky. And one day, in the middle of the night, instead of texting me, he called me.

"I need you to tell me something, my Torment. I need to hear you say it."

"Whatever you need."

"Do you love me?"

"Yes." My heart had never beaten like this before. As if all the drums of Calanda were trapped under my ribs. Men's knuckles bleeding against the taut leather. With all their strength. All at once during the darkest hours of the night.

"I need you to say it so I can believe you. I'm taking too much risk. I could lose everything for you."

I hesitated. The words were right there, waiting on my tongue, but my chest shrank and wouldn't let them out. There was a seemingly eternal silence.

"Torment—"

"I love you."

"You would never betray me, would you?"

"Never."

And then he said it. And it destroyed me forever.

"I love you, too."

ESTELA

Eva takes me by the hand into Coral's forest. We go barefoot and the grass under our feet is soft and warm. Eva smiles, she talks to me, but I don't understand what she says. We are naked, my hair loose and the red brooch dancing on my chest. The sun bathes my skin. We reach the end of the path and arrive in front of a majestic oak tree. Coral is sitting on its branches with her face hidden. Eva lets go of my hand. She has left me alone.

Coral is a girl, as in the photos in the dossier. She is crying. Curled up on the ground. I approach to comfort her, but when I put my hand on her shoulder and she lifts her head to look at me, her eyes are two uneven stones stitched together with red thread. She opens her mouth to speak, or to scream, but as she does, a pile of soggy leaves, worms and dirt comes out of her throat with a sound like walking through the woods in autumn. I try to move away from her, but my feet are roots sinking deeper and deeper into the ground. Coral stands up, dripping that blackish mixture from her lips. Her hands are no longer those of a child, but the nails blend into the skin, stretched, sharp and blackened. They are dry, twisted, pointed branches. Her breasts burst into mushrooms. She digs her nails into my bulging belly, cutting it from side to side. I want to scream, but I can't. Something is caught in my throat. Something moving, running across my tongue. Hundreds of spiders swarm in my mouth, choking me, not letting me scream. Coral's hands dig into my belly. I feel no pain. Finally, her hands withdraw. It is not a baby she's holding. It is not human. She lifts it, but I can't get a good look. There is hair where there should be skin. I want to see better. I try to reach up to take it from her. My breasts fill with milk. I can almost see it. Round, black eyes ...

But I can never finish the dream. I never find out what Coral rips out of my belly. I can't figure out what it means. Eva would have some irrational theory. Maybe her theories weren't so absurd after all.

I would give anything to hear her crazy ideas again.

God, I would give anything.

Anything.

INTERVIEW_CRL_DAY_NINE.mp4

EVA: It's only been a week, but I have very good news, Coral, would you like to know? You are the first person I am going to share it with. We haven't even told the family.

CORAL: We already know, sweet girl. Estela is pregnant. It was what was promised.

EVA: Yes, yesterday the gynecologist confirmed the test result. I am sure it will be a girl. Estela says we don't have to get excited, that we can't tell anyone until the first trimester is over, but I know it will be fine, and that the girl will be fierce, strong, like you said. The girl I saw as a swallow from the window.

CORAL: Of course, we have never lied to you, have we?

EVA: No. [Whispers] I did what you told me, and now the doll is under the bed. I don't understand how that's possible, though. The truth is I don't want to try to understand it. I have never been so happy.

CORAL: There is nothing to understand. She likes you. She wants to fulfill your wishes. Soon you'll see her and you'll have to give her a name. Have you thought of one?

[Cut]

EVA: How would you feel if I told you that I have found Raúl Expósito? That these are not suppositions, that I can prove it?

CORAL: I would say that you are crazy, and that you are confused. Because if he were alive, then, Ayalga still owes me a debt, I could still offer her something else in exchange for his return to me.

EVA: I need you to tell me what happened next to understand why you are reluctant to think you might be wrong.

CORAL

Raúl made me believe I was his girlfriend. A secret one, but his anyway. So I behaved accordingly. One morning I walked into the girls' bathroom. I had seen him in the hallway restroom, so I made sure to pass him on my way, when everyone was closing the classroom doors. I made sure no one was in the cubicles and a minute later, just as I expected, Raúl walked into the bathroom. He pushed me into one of the stalls and slammed me against the wall.

"What do you think you're doing? Huh?" He wasn't happy, he was angry. Angry with me. I couldn't understand why. "You want to get me fired? You want to send me to jail? Why are you tormenting me like this?"

I couldn't understand why he was so angry.

"No, of course not," I whimpered.

"People talk. They talk about us. You have to get a boyfriend, so the rumors stop." He looked at me very seriously.

For a moment, I thought he would hit me. That he would leave me. I feared him like the first time I heard his firm voice over the phone. I tried to move closer to kiss him, I couldn't think of any other way to calm him down. He pulled away. He wouldn't let me kiss him, offered me no kindness. I was trembling. Scared. Heartbroken. As if I had been abandoned on the street, naked and helpless.

"Get a boyfriend, or consider it over," he said, carefully opening the door and checking that we were still alone.

He was leaving, when I leaned over the door and asked, "But who?"

"I don't give a shit who," he replied without looking at me.

I didn't question it. I didn't think twice about it. Just as I had participated in his games, I followed his orders in this regard. Ayalga would have exactly what I needed to accomplish this new task and make Raúl happy and mine again.

That night my phone vibrated on my bedside table. It was a message from Raúl. The loving and attentive Raúl.

"I'm sorry for what happened today. I want us to be together, but we can't risk everything, my love. People wouldn't understand, that's why it's important that everyone thinks you have a boyfriend. What have you done to me? I've never felt this before, I know it's wrong, but something bad doesn't feel like this, does it? You're my sweet Torment," he explained.

I wanted to be his Torment, not one more in the long line of girls he tricked into loving him.

Tony_Lorenzo.mp4

EVA: I can only imagine how difficult it must have been for you back then, and now, I want to thank you again for doing this. I gathered that you were a shy kid in high school.

TONY: Yes, I guess I was. I remember mostly that I felt as lonely as Coral. That was the main reason I liked her. I was in love with her since, well, since forever. I used to be one of her brother's targets when he was the local bully. I lived in the same village, and I knew she never had any interest in me. I was content to admire her from afar. I was too afraid of Señor Magia since we were kids.

EVA: She testified at the trial about how you started dating. What was your reaction when the bodies were found?

TONY: It was shocking and heartbreaking, you know? I was an ordinary teenager with a boring life. The most exciting thing that had ever happened to me was dating

Coral.

First, I learned my girlfriend was in the
hospital, that a madman had broken into
her house and killed everyone and hurt
her. That alone would have been enough
to fuck with anyone's head, don't you
think? I was devastated.

My mother used to take me to the hospital to visit her when she was in
that medically induced coma. She had
no one else. They were all dead. The
Guardia Civil started asking all those
questions and she woke up. And she didn't
want to see me. She kicked me out of
her room. The Guardia Civil asked to
take blood and saliva samples from me.
I swore I was a virgin, and I didn't
even know she had been pregnant. I had
never seen her naked. But they didn't
care. If the baby was delivered, they
wanted to make sure I wasn't the father.
When I found out the rest. God ... It's
still so hard to believe, you know, I
could never have said she was pregnant.
Not that delusional. She never told me
anything that would make me suspicious.
Raúl Expósito was a good teacher. He

didn't behave particularly well with her, nor did he give her different attention. Honestly, I was crazy about Coral, but that guy was dating Lorena Bazán. That woman was like a goddess to us. Besides, did you see pictures of him? I'd give my arm to look anything like him, he didn't have to chase girls or rape them. They never found the baby, did they?

EVA: No, they didn't. You'd be surprised to know what some attractive men are capable of. [Sighs] Did you ever feel in danger around her?

TONY: Danger? No, not at all. I mean. Even the dog was nice to me when we first started dating. Look, you have to understand, she was the love of my life and I've never been happier than those months we were together.

EVA: Would you like to hear what she has to say about how you started dating?

TONY: I guess so. Yes.

CORAL

The next day, in the cafeteria during lunch, I grabbed two bottles of soda and took them to the bathroom. I opened one and spit into it a mixture of my saliva, sap and chewed leaves. Then I closed it and went back outside. I found Tony in the library, where I usually went instead of eating lunch alone in the cafeteria. I had learned that this was the best way to avoid guys like Carlos. They never set foot in the library anyway. I sat down next to him.

"Hi, Tony," I whispered. "You thirsty?" I said, offering him the bottle. "I bought one for you too."

I smiled at the boy who couldn't believe this was happening. I had never spoken to him in our years together at school or as neighbors.

He tried to speak but couldn't find the words. I put the bottle in his hand, stroking his fingers as if by chance, although it was a very studied movement. He drank. And just like that he was ours. Mine and Ayalga's.

From that day on, we sat together on the train. And we walked into school holding hands. Raúl was once again behaving like the love of my life. Tony, he was a gentleman, if only because he was under my spell. Nothing he did when he went out with me was his idea or desire. I probably could have gotten the guy without charming him, but it comforted me to control his adolescent urges. I didn't plan to kiss him, and the thought of his tongue moving inside my mouth repulsed me. I also thought Raúl would be jealous if we behaved like a couple when people weren't looking at us.

Tony_Lorenzo.mp4

TONY: That's not what I remember. Not at all. Honestly, I don't know why she would say those things or why she did what she did. We kissed. We kissed *a lot*. And she told me she loved me. More than once. I ... this is too much, could we ... could we stop, please? I need a minute.

ESTELA

There is a locked drawer in the desk. I didn't even know this desk had a locked drawer. I go to the kitchen and return with a knife. Fortunately, whoever made these drawers did not intend for State secrets to be kept in them. The wood and the lock give way immediately to my onslaught with the butter knife.

I *don't* want to find something in here. I want my suspicions to be unfounded. I want the xanas not to exist. But I cannot retrace this road I have traveled. This certainty that we would never have been mothers if Coral had not entered our lives. If Raúl Expósito were dead.

I sit on the floor with the crate between my spread legs. The child, this spawn of the forest nesting in my womb, takes up too much space inside me to cross my legs or sit comfortably. Inside the drawer is only a shoebox with the running shoes Eva gave me two years ago when we promised we were going to get in shape by going for a run and we never delivered.

I open the box and my breath catches.

On one of my winter pajamas rests a rag doll, although doll would be too flattering a name for this thing. I pick it up in my hands but drop it with a jerk. I've pricked myself with something, as if it were stuffed with thorns and needles. The girl stirs inside me. I scrutinize the doll and the skin on the back of my neck prickles. The red curls resemble my own. Too much so. I pick up the doll again, carefully so I don't hurt myself. It smells like my shampoo and this hair is not artificial. It has two green stones sewn with a red thread and worn in the shape of a cross. I squeeze it and it rustles like it's stuffed with dry leaves. It's crooked and obnoxious, but there's no doubt it's me.

Under the doll I find an envelope.

Estela

I recognize Eva's careful handwriting. Although shaky.

"I have made a very serious mistake. It's not the kind of mistake that can be fixed by talking, or with help. I didn't know I was putting you in danger. We wanted so badly to get it right this time. I know you must have hated me for what I'm about to do, but I'm sure by the time you find this note, you'll have figured it all out. You will already know that this is my only hope to keep you both safe. Forgive me. Take care of our daughter. I love you."

Damn you, Eva. I didn't want this child. I didn't want to be a mother. I wanted you, stupid. If you'd paid attention ...

I take the doll and the jar with the herbal tea then go out to the inner courtyard of our house loaded with a box full to the brim and the metal garbage can from Eva's office.

I take Coral's case files out of the box, tear up the sheets of paper and throw them into the wastebasket. Her notes. The photographs. I throw away the doll, empty the contents of the jar. I take the matches out of my dungarees pocket. I light one and place the flame on the protruding papers. I light several corners. The fire begins to devour the contents of the garbage can. Pieces of burning paper fly across the yard. Coral's photographs are consumed.

The doll writhes in the flames with a tea kettle scream. The seams of her eyes give way, releasing the stones. Her curls sizzle.

A prick so intense as to make me double over in pain pierces my belly.

Special Episode of THE GARDEN OF HORRORS: A True Crime Company Podcast

Aired on July 7, 2018 as an introduction to episode #5

I'm Jennifer Montes, *co-host* of The Garden of Horrors. Last Saturday we were not punctual to our appointment, and we debated a lot before deciding to continue with the podcast.

Most of you who are listening to us know why.

Ten years after the crimes committed by Coral López Ramos, our colleague Eva Villar decided that True Crime Company would carry out a series of episodes about her family's crimes. In the first interview with Coral, she discovered so many things. She even recorded all the episodes that would be broadcasted, but she only lived to listen to the first four.

The body of our colleague, my friend Eva,

was found hanged in the same forest as the corpses of this macabre series of crimes the morning of June 25th of this year. With the tape recorder at her feet. We know she was alone, that no one is to blame for her death. Eva decided to take her own life that day.

I wish we had known what she was planning to do. I wish we could have helped her. Her widow, Estela Gómez, has given us permission to continue with the podcast. She and the whole team think that if she had left a note, if she had been able to express her last wish, it would have been to continue.

Eva, sit tibi terra levis.

[The Bear Dance, acoustic version]

I'm Eva Villar, and this is The Garden of Horrors, a True Crime Company podcast. Welcome to Episode Five.

The relationship progressed slowly. Small steps during the nights, while during the day they were nothing more than teacher and student. Coral felt Raúl

Expósito's claw in her chest, squeezing her throat, dominating her will complete- ly. She lost her senses, her sanity. There was nothing but that love. At the same time, she could not help but feel uncomfortable. It was an oppressive feeling. Unbearable.

Tony would pick her up and walk with her, Carlos and Señor Magia to the station every day. She called them during in- terviews on several occasions "my little cohort of forest gifts." And I guess that's what they were, after all.▨

Her obsession with Raúl Expósito grew even more when rumors began to spread that he was dating Miss Bazán, the His- tory teacher Coral tells us about in this excerpt from our interviews.

Listener discretion is advised. Some descriptions may be disturbing.

CORAL

Miss Bazán had been my favorite teacher since I started high school. She was our youngest teacher and was certainly a brilliant woman. From my point of view, she was a role model.

She had explained the witch hunts in Spain in a way no other teacher had. We devoted a couple of classes to studying the only witch ever executed in the region. No one ever mentioned her. They pretended it had only been a U.S. problem. A virus contained in the city of Salem. It was almost as if that teacher wanted us to celebrate dead women as a result of superstition.

One day she brought a T-shirt to class that said, *We are the granddaughters of the witches you couldn't burn.*

And I went crazy for her.

She spoke of healing with natural remedies, of gossip as a useful tool to help the community. She noticed my interest in the subject and offered an interesting bibliography I devoured like a wolf at the end of winter.

I wanted to be like Miss Bazán when I grew up, so it was even more painful to discover that *my Raúl* was interested in her. That it was reciprocated. That Lorena Bazán had become the official girlfriend.

They both betrayed me. I went mad with rage, became ill with it. I spent days in bed in a strange fever, oozing sap from the pores of my skin that left me sticky as if I had bathed in honey.

When I saw them talking in the hallways, a chunk of ice stabbed my heart. I know it sounds cliché, but I couldn't describe it better. Besides, I know what it feels like to have something stuck in your chest, don't I?

One night, I couldn't deal with my feelings anymore. They were overflowing like a forgotten pot on the stove. I snuck out of the house, through the village and up the road in the dark with Señor Magia following me to the door of my love. The one I had seen while flying over the village as a raven on my oak sap travels.

It was a two-story house with a pink bougainvillea climbing up the wall. It was rare. Most were lilac, dark, purple. His were pale and delicate. A wooden corridor crossed the facade and looked out over the valley. The openwork walls were painted dark red. It was the house I wanted to build my home in. The home that Lorena Bazán was stealing from me.

Years of sneaking around at night had given me the experience to avoid unwelcome glances. I stood silently by the dark wooden door, carved with Celtic symbols, very still like a small viper in tall grass.

I walked around the house I had never been invited to and looked into the living room window. The night air was cold and smelled of rain. Inside, the burning fireplace made the walls dance with orange tones, music from the mountains was playing, very soft. A light scent of vanilla drifted into my mouth from the open window. Raúl and Miss Bazán were curled up on the sofa drinking wine, laughing. The perfect night I had imagined for myself. Why wasn't I with him? It was one thing to have a fake boyfriend, a cover, because he ordered me to, and another thing entirely to be cuddling on the couch with another woman. I pulled out my phone and texted him.

"What's that bitch doing in there? I'm outside. Get her out of your house NOW!"

I didn't think about the consequences of that text message. Of making my presence known at the window. I hadn't thought about what his reaction might be. Submerged in my own rage, jealousy had the same flavor of magic.

Raúl picked up his phone. Slightly uncomfortable, he withdrew his arm from around the *other's* body, excused himself and headed for the kitchen. Lorena lay on the couch, smiling to herself like a stupid little girl. *Look at you, what a role model.*

"Are you out of your mind or what?" he whispered, albeit with the tone of an angry shout, when he opened the door. With a quick, dry movement he pushed me into the bushes. Pressed against the cold wall at the corner of his house, where darkness enveloped us out of reach of the neighbors' eyes.

"What the hell is *she* doing here?" I wanted to mutter, but my voice came out too loud.

I didn't mind that he covered my mouth with his hand. That big, soft hand as if he had never worked a minute in his life. It was a hard squeeze. It hurt around my jaw. The teeth pressed against the inside of my lips. Throbbing. The familiar, coppery taste of blood brimmed in my mouth.

I had never felt that kind of fear.

That was the day I realized I was completely in his hands. At his mercy. It terrified me, yes. But I'd be lying if I didn't say it also set off a torrent of desire between my legs.

"How can you be so stupid? What do you think?" He got even angrier. "It's none of your business what I do, you'd do well to remember that the next time you want to make a scene."

Regret slid down my back like rain soaking into my bones. I had made him angry. I had doubted him. Maybe I would lose him after that night. I kissed his hand with my bruised lips and wept, wetting his skin. My knees were barely holding me up.

I am ashamed of this, but if he had wanted to kill me at that moment, I doubt I would have put up much of a fight. Not only my body, but my mind was his. Completely his.

He must have realized I had let go, that I was at his feet completely, because he pushed me further into the shadows. He pinned me against the wall and reached inside my pants. Inside my underwear. At no time did he loosen the hand that held my mouth firmly shut. My voice trapped.

He did not kiss me.

He said nothing.

He just gazed longingly into my red, watery eyes and licked the tears that rolled down his hand. It was the first time he had caressed my skin. We had only kissed once. I had masturbated thinking about him a few nights. It wasn't even a regular thing. I had felt Ayalga's mystical touch, half skin, half wood, but no man had ever touched my sex before. I was angry, terrified, excited. I trembled like branches driven mad by the chestnut wind. My heart was racing. My head was spinning. I was wet, tender, I closed my eyes and let myself be carried away by his touch.

It was not at all how I had imagined it. His fingers were not as efficient as hers, nor mine. He was too rough. Too eager. He was squeezing and hurting me. But I let him do it. He was older. More experienced. He knew what he was doing, didn't he? My eyes locked on his. It was that look, not the awkward movement of his hands that ignited my body. A warm pleasure creeped into my navel as I remembered the words Ayalga had whispered to me:

"Give in. Let yourself go."

My body slowly adjusted to the new reality of that other skin on mine. Raúl stopped abruptly. Leaving me lost, suspended over the sea of my own desire. Anxious, agitated. I let out a moan against the palm of his hand that never let go of my mouth.

"What have you turned me into? God, I love you so much that I can't contain myself when I'm near you. You are my Torment," he whispered in my ear.

I felt powerful. As ridiculous as it may seem now. I did. Like a goddess, like he was on his knees, impotent from my presence. I was the reason he was hiding in the dark touching me, losing his mind instead of being inside, warm and safe in Lorena's arms.

"I have to go. My Torment."

I nodded, and he finally released my face.

"We'll find a way to be together, you'll see," he said before kissing me. "Now go home before anyone sees you."

I ran without looking back, followed by Señor Magia who had not moved from my side, but neither had he tried to defend me. My whole body was shaking. I ran upstairs and threw myself on the bed. I was going to love him forever. Until death and beyond. I was his Torment. I gulped down every word as if I had been fed with milk and flower honey.

Until my heart stopped beating it would be his.

Until the night sky turned white.

Until my skin turned to ashes.

Nothing Raúl said changed the fact that, right then, when I was awake and alone on the bed, they were together. Were they lying like I was lying on the bed? Was he touching her like he had touched me? Did she like it? I had to take care of Miss Bazán.

I got up and ran into the forest. I leaned my full weight against the tree trunk, full of anger, my eyes blazing.

"Show me what to do," I begged, trying to dig my nails into the oak, to hurt her so she would understand how serious it was. "Show me how to get her away from him."

The temperature plummeted. The wind blew through my hair as if combing it, caring for me like a mother. The roots of the oak tree opened and from the darkness of the earth emerged her green eyes, round, without a hint of white in them. They shone with a light of their own, like fireflies. She smiled, and from her lips dripped fresh, sweet mountain water. She clutched at the bark of the tree with long, sharp, blackened fingers and climbed out of her hole in the ground like a spider.

"Feed on me and it will be her blood that is poisoned. They will never be together again," she uttered.

I fell to my knees and nodded. Ayalga, standing in front of me, grabbed a handful of dirt and shoved it into my mouth, which was waiting openly for that twisted communion. I suppressed a retch before swallowing it whole. She grabbed another, and another. And another. Dry leaves, broken twigs, worms, ants. I kept swallowing and swallowing as if to fill a void that only grew as I tried to cover it up.

I had never seen anything more beautiful than her. No matter how many times I, the mushrooms sprouting from her cracked skin, the greenish moss covered with tiny flowers on her skull, on her pubis. I wanted and needed her as much as a breath of air in the middle of the ocean. I ran my hands gently down her legs. Her skin was cold and rough as the trunk. I ventured my fingers slowly into the moss growing wild between her legs, enjoying her tremors, feeling the forest moisture warm inside her.

I swallowed another handful of mud before she reached over and pressed her wet, greenish sex against my open mouth bursting with passion.

From: lbazan@iesespina.com
To: evavillar@truepod.com

Subject: Re: Re: Re: Re: Podcast interview

Hello Eva,

I'm glad we were able to come to an agreement and that you respect my decision. I pasted in the body of the email the annotations I made, I hope they will help you for the podcast. I still don't think it's a good idea, but I respect your reasons and hope you get what you set out to do.

Best regards,
Lorena

Raúl Expósito and I started dating shortly after he arrived at the center. We kept it a secret for the first few months, just in case it didn't work out. Actually, it was my idea. He said he didn't care, that he was sure about us and that it wouldn't affect our work. He was a sweet man and never pressured me to go too fast. I won't go into details, and I hope you won't include this, but some episodes in my past make it difficult to feel comfortable in intimate situations. He was patient. And we didn't have sex until I was completely ready. He was always sweet and loving.

When we finally went public with our relationship, Coral began to tease me in class. She was a straight-A student who suddenly hated me. Raúl was aware of her feelings for him as we talked about it on several occasions, but there wasn't much we could do. It happens when you work with teenagers. All those feelings are new and hard to control.

But Coral was different. She was not like other girls. I'm from a town in Galicia, and as they say about the *meigas*, *haberlas hailas*. They do exist. Coral proved it to me the hard way.

That afternoon, Raúl and I were at his house when Coral showed up at his door unexpectedly. It's not normal for a student to go to a teacher's house. She made a scene. I heard her from the living room. They were arguing. Raúl tried to calm her down. I decided to wait inside thinking if I intervened it would be worse. Finally, he got her to calm down and leave.

When he came back, we tried to keep her from ruining our evening. I'm embarrassed to say it, but we may have been laughing a little at her. At her crush. At the little outburst of jealousy. I was taking a sip of wine next to Raúl when the vomit came unexpectedly. Mud began to drip

from my lips, sticks ripped
my throat, leaves, worm. It
gushed uncontrollably, without spasms in my stomach or
my body making any effort to
expel it.

I fell to my knees and tried
to stop the earth that fled
from my bowels in violent
bursts. It spilled equally
between my open hands. I
could not breathe. The smell
of dampness, of rot filled
everything. I was drowning as
if submerged in a swamp without having left Raúl's living room. There is no worse
feeling than struggling for
air when it surrounds you in
abundance.

Raúl didn't know how to help
me. I lost track of where I
was. Ten years have passed,
and I still dream that I'm
there, but it's not me. I see
myself on all fours covering
his carpet with all that bit-

ter earth.

Raúl never saw me naked
again. We never went out
again. I don't blame him. How
could he see me and not think
of maggots tumbling from my
lips? I know it was her. I
knew it when I was in the
hospital and the news came
out. I was sure of it. There
was nothing natural about
what happened to me. Nothing
human. That girl is a savage.
A demon.

CORAL

On the first day of spring, I ran away from home. It was my birthday, but this year, like so many before, there was no cartoon costume. No big twin cakes. I wanted to share my birthday with Raúl. I was going to give him my most prized possession. The doll Ayalga had given me when I was still a little girl.

The rags she was made of hadn't aged at all since the day I dug her out of the forest. Her expression was the same. The lock of hair still smelled like the shampoo Marisa bought us when we were kids. As I smelled the doll, the hot chocolate, the shampoo, the churros and the cinnamon, I was filled with memories of my childhood. Of the time when everything was simple and easy. Before blood. Before love. Before I became the Torment. It also smelled of the forest. Raw and strong. It was the perfect blend of the two of us.

I walked back down the road to Raúl's house. Only this time he had invited me and had taken every precaution not to get caught. I wrapped the doll in a piece of my clothes that I had slept in for a whole week, so that it would have even more of my essence. I had bought myself a woman's dress, red lipstick and liquid eyeliner, like the ones Miss Bazán wore. I looked at myself in the mirror and recognized Aunt Olvido's beauty in my own features.

He greeted me at his house through the back door. It was obvious from the look on his face that he didn't appreciate the outfit or the makeup.

"Why are you dressed up?"

"Never have I ever dressed for a date?" I said almost in a whisper, terribly embarrassed.

That calmed his nerves. He closed the door behind me. He held me by the waist.

"You don't need all that, because you're already perfect. I want to see your naked, unadulterated beauty. Would you go upstairs and wipe your face for me?"

As confused as I was, I still thought of it as a compliment. Other women needed to disguise their imperfections, but not me. My pubescent skin was perfect for him.

In the bathroom I smelled his towels. His aftershave. I cleaned my face with warm water and soap, but the red lipstick was so strong and thick that my lips were swollen from the effort. It looked like I had been crying. I went back downstairs. All the windows were closed, the only light inside came from the fireplace.

"Now, perfect," he said looking at me with a glass of red wine in his hand. "Come sit with me," he invited me with eagerness in his voice.

Trembling with fear and desire, I sat beside him. He offered me a sip of his wine. I tasted it. It was bitter. I didn't like it, but I didn't want it to show. He laughed at my obvious effort. I felt small and stupid.

"I brought you a gift," I said, trying to regain control of my nerves. "It's something very important to me. I've had it since I was a little girl and now I want you to have it. There is nothing more precious to me that I can give you," I concluded, taking the doll out of my backpack and placing the package in his hands.

He set the wine glass aside, and with a condescending look unwrapped my gift.

"A doll. Very metaphorical, I expected nothing less from a poet like you."

I wasn't sure if he was making fun of me or really liked me.

"The resemblance is uncanny, did your mother make it?" he asked, looking at the doll's face, smelling her hair.

"No, it was ... no," I answered without finding the words.

What would he think of me if I told him the truth about myself? Would he realize it had been me who provoked Miss Bazán's incident? Would he behave like the men in the witch burnings? Or would he be sympathetic? I didn't want to find out yet. We would have all our lives. I could ease his way little by little.

"I'll keep it next to me in bed, so you can be with me every night." He kissed the doll and put it on the table next to the glass of wine. I smiled.

Then he leaned over me and started kissing me.

"Now, what other gifts are you going to offer me tonight?"

Sex was nothing like I had imagined in my long nights. Nothing like what I had experienced in the forest. I expected to tremble with passion and pleasure. I expected it to take me to heaven and hell and all the way back. I imagined tender caresses, beauty, my heart exploding with unimaginable love. Everything the magic of the forest made me feel ten times over.

But it didn't even come close.

Raúl's hands on my skin were rough. Urgent. Violent. He undressed me carelessly. He hurried. He didn't even undress completely. I could feel everything around me. I was nervous and not wet enough. The firelight hurt my eyes. The fabric of the couch was too rough. The elastic band of the socks he didn't take off squeezed. His fingernails. His teeth. His penis hard against my stomach at first. His hands clumsily firm on my sex. I should have felt love, but instead I was terrified. I couldn't distinguish the tinkling at the back of my spine when he touched me from that of opening my gums to offer my tooth to the forest. Both a price of admission to forbidden pleasures. Only, on this occasion, the pleasure never came.

"Let me in, come on, my Torment," he whispered in my ear as his fingers tried to slide into my dry pussy. He pulled his hand out and spat on it. Then he coated my sex with his saliva, and without warning he thrust inside me in one firm lunge. The pain of that stab was retroactive. It took a second for my nerves to feel it. And before I could scream, he covered my mouth with his hands as he had done the day I showed up at his door unannounced.

He was moving inside me. Hurting me. His sweat covered my face. It dripped into my eyes. It filled my mouth with a salty taste that was unfamiliar to me. His animal-like moans made me uncomfortable. There was nothing left of the gentleman I loved in that beast. My body went numb. It was a relief. He let out a moan and stopped. He pulled out of me and showered me with kisses.

"Most girls don't come the first time, don't worry.

So it was my fault. I should have enjoyed it. I was a disappointment.

"I'm sorry," I apologized.

"Next time you will," he said, looking into my eyes. "God, you're so beautiful. I've never seen anyone drive me so crazy—"

"Did I bleed?" I asked, concerned about the upholstery of his couch.

He looked down.

"No, maybe there's something you haven't told me about that jerk Tony Lorenzo," he laughed at me.

I was disappointed by the lack of blood. Blood had always marked the great moments of my life, and it was not part of this, the most significant one. My first time with the love of my life. Have you ever noticed that when you're in love, it's always about the love of your life?

From then on it was all love and tenderness. Although it was brief, as I had to leave early. I left the doll behind. My thighs ached when I walked.

Carlos and Señor Magia were waiting for me on the porch. I didn't know why I wanted to cry. But I let myself go and sat between them, hugging them and pouring out all the mixture of my feelings.

It was like a cleanse.

Guillermo was getting ready for bed when he heard the crying. He opened the door. We looked at him. He opened his mouth as if to speak. Lost in his own thoughts. He looked at us and left us there, hugging.

"She would have known what to do," he muttered as he climbed the stairs.

I was convinced that this could not be all. Raúl was the love of my life and that first experience with him had not a shred of magic.

"Why are you crying, my sweet girl?" Ayalga asked me when I ran to her side that night.

I could not collect my thoughts enough to produce words. Just babbling and tears. Ayalga came closer. We were so close to each other her breath infected mine. Her sharp hands reached under my shirt and brushed against my breasts. I got goose bumps, and my nipples ached as they hardened. Her fingers went even further, sinking into my skin. It hurt, but not enough to scream and beg for her to stop. They were sneaking in between my ribs and moving forward. The pressure in my chest made it hard to breathe. Finally, her claws cold as river water embraced my heart. Squeezing it as if it if juicing a fresh fruit. I was lost in her strange, beautiful eyes as I felt myself dying in her arms. Finally, she smiled and the pressure disappeared as she withdrew her hands covered in bright red blood. As she licked her fingers, I pressed my hands to my chest, searching for the open wound.

"What would you be willing to give for him to love you until his heart stops?"

"Even the last drop of my blood."

"Blood of your blood and flesh of your flesh?"

"Anything. There is nothing, no life, that I am not willing to sacrifice in return."

ESTELA

"No heartbeat."

Two words. Three syllables. What a brief incantation to devastate the world. I shouldn't have burned my doll. I shouldn't have stopped taking the tea. Damn it, I shouldn't have believed all that nonsense about xanas and magic.

The doctor talks while I wipe off the ultrasound gel. I must pay close attention to my options. Understand everything she says. But my brain is going too fast, unable to form a coherent thought. My knees shake as I stand up.

Have I lost them both?

"There is no hurry. Go home. Call someone. Read this brochure. Rest over the weekend and come back on Monday."

Perinatal death. What now? The rounded pastel-colored letters of the brochure curl around my chest like a python leaving me breathless. The doctor points to a particular page.

"Look, this is the part you have to read. There is everything I have told you, and if you have more questions, you can call this number here. It is an association that helps people through this process. For now, just monitor your fever. If it goes up, come to the emergency room immediately, okay?"

I nod as I get up to leave. I should call someone.

Eva.

It's been more than five months since her body was nothing but ashes and still that's the first thought that assails me. By the time I realize it, I'm already home. My feet are floating. At the same time, I have never felt so heavy. I lie down on the couch and put my hands on my bulging belly. I pull them away, startled, realizing I am caressing a heart that no longer beats.

"I am a coffin."

My stomach shrinks. My throat is knotted. I grab my cell phone to call the doctor, overwhelmed by the need to tear her away from me as soon as possible. To get rid of her body. Of her weight in my belly. I contemplate my possibilities according to the brochure. An oxytocin-induced labor when I deem it appropriate. Or wait. Expectant management, they call it. My body will figure out what has happened. It will try to get rid of the child on its own. *Like a normal labor*. Normal. As if such a thing has existed since Eva hanged herself from that tree. I also have to decide if I want to see the baby, spend time with her. With her lifeless body.

I spent so many nights imagining the child born covered in moss and mushrooms, that it did not occur to me, that perhaps, if I took her to Coral's forest and gave her to the xana of the tree, Eva's body would rise from the earth. Without the horrible make-up she wore to the crematorium. It only occurred to me that was the meaning of it all when I heard those two words.

No heartbeat.

In fiction, pure love, the real good kind, can achieve anything. Even that. With no jolts this time, I stroke my belly. Closing my eyes, I embrace the absurd idea of pretending nothing has changed. I hide the pamphlet under the couch cushions. Nothing that confirms the certainty that death is an irreversible process is welcome here in my realm of ashes.

Calling someone seems impossible right now. I don't want pity, even more so. How will they look at me now that I'm not just a widow? They'll look at me like I'm the saddest woman in the universe.

I just want a gazpacho. Yes. That's what I want. Put on some music and make me a gazpacho like it was yesterday. As if the words *no heartbeat* had never been uttered. Undo those two words. Practice a spell that would change this dead baby into a living *xanino* with which to bring Eva back to life.

When I was little, my grandmother always kept a jar of fresh gazpacho in the fridge. When I moved out of my parents' house, she gave me a recipe notebook written in her round, childlike handwriting. Though I know how to make it, I always take the notebook out and put it on the counter next to the vegetables. The pages are stamped with tomato and garlic flowers from my fingerprints after chopping the ingredients. I start with the cucumber, garlic and green bell pepper. The smell of the vegetables floods the kitchen. I chop the tomatoes while humming a copla my grandmother loved. *I'll stick glass pins in my eyes, so I won't see myself face to face, with you and your truth.*

Rage invades me as I think of all those people who don't deserve the air they breathe, the space they waste. The annoying neighbor across the street we can't get rid of. My miserable boss ...

Eva made the world a better place.

A cut on my finger brings me back to reality. My body is still mine. The pain reminds me that I am not a wooden coffin, that I am still little more than flesh and bones. I instinctively stick my bloody finger in my mouth as I search for a Band-Aid in the bathroom. The metallic taste overwhelms my senses. I stop in my tracks. A spark. A small shock. An absurd idea, but so strong that I am unable to resist it.

I take out the urn with Eva's ashes and mix half of it with the gazpacho.

If you're not coming back, at least make us one.

I swallow the thick, lumpy liquid that has lost its bright red color to become a fading brown.

A kick.

"Girl?"

Nothing.

But I'm sure I felt it. I take another gulp, drink breathlessly straight from the blender glass until there's not a drop left. A crisp, clear thought is etched in my mind. A certainty I cannot ignore. I hope.

There it is.

Stretching. Untangling her limbs inside me. Now I cry. I allow myself to because they are not tears of sorrow. Because I feel her more than ever. How she is now, still in my belly, and how she will be. Green eyes, singing voice and skin mixed with moss. A waterfall between teeth of rocks. Small hands. Light feet.

I have no doubt.

I do not tremble.

Immersed in this new certainty, however irrational it may seem, I know that I will get the love of my life back.

CORAL

"Come to my village and follow my street. You will see an old fence, broken towards the end. Go through it. I have gone in there so many times you will see my path on the ground. Look for me under the big old oak tree," I wrote.

"Do you really call this a forest, honey?" Raúl sent a message when he arrived at the spot. I had a hard time convincing him to have that date, I guess he was already planning his escape, but finally, he couldn't resist one last bite.

Of course, I called it a forest. It was my forest. The most sacred place on Earth. He would see it soon enough.

Raúl was standing casually leaning against the old oak tree, smoking a cigarette. I don't think she liked that. Maybe I should have told him not to smoke here. Not to touch the tree before I got here. He was desecrating my kingdom, but I said nothing when he flicked the lit butt and pressed it to the ground with his boot.

"Hello, my sweet Torment, are you sure you want to be here? It's a bit cold," he said.

"Oh, yeah?" I added as the forest air warmed once I filled it with my presence.

He smiled and raised his eyebrows in confusion. I hugged him. He pressed me against his chest and smelled my hair deeply. Then we kissed slowly. An army of insects scoured my stomach and thighs. My sex tinkled and became wet. He pressed me against the old oak tree and the magic and the forest became a swamp.

That night, even surrounded by my own magic, was no better. Is it ever? I often wondered. His moans in my ear did not match what I experienced. Once again, I had expected love. Pleasure. I got darkness. Pain. Tears. His beard scratched the soft skin on my chest. The rough dirt under my back made little cuts. Mosquitoes fed on my bare legs.

Raúl was still inside me when I tilted my head and saw Carlos and Señor Magia watching us from a safe distance. Their somber gazes in the darkness stabbed my mind.

I was embarrassed.

I closed my eyes. I cried silently, and when I opened them Ayalga was in front of me. Raúl was not aware of her presence.

"It's done, my sweet girl," she murmured.

She stroked my hair and licked the tears falling from my eyes with a scratchy cat-like tongue.

"It has already happened. It's already growing inside of you. Our deal is sealed."

Raúl gave me a kiss on the cheek and stood up. He zipped his pants before helping me stand. We walked in silence to the edge of the forest.

"You go first," he said. "I know the way home, no one must see us together."

I nodded. Then I hugged him tightly. He laughed and kissed me.

"Don't think too much about me," he said with a kiss on my forehead.

INTERVIEW_CLR_DAY10.mp4

EVA: What happened next, when did you find out you were pregnant, and did you tell him?

CORAL: I knew it the very instant it happened. Ayalga told me. It was what she wanted, so I had no doubt there was something growing inside me. On Monday, he didn't even look at me. Not that I expected things to have changed. After all, we were still teacher and student, but at least I expected a message. A look, a wink. Something. But it didn't happen. I sent him messages in the afternoon and evening, but he didn't answer them.

EVA: Not a word?

CORAL: Nothing. Tuesday morning, when I opened the street door to go to school, there was a package on the step. A shoebox wrapped in brown paper. Señor Magia was sniffing it and wagging his tail in delight. Carlos put his hand on my shoulder as if he already knew what was inside, as if he wanted to comfort me beforehand because my heart was about to be broken.

We put the box inside. It didn't matter if we were going to miss the train. I placed the package on the kitchen table, not daring to open it yet. I was trying to prolong the moment. If I didn't open it, it wasn't true. As long as the package was closed, my world had not yet gone to pieces. If I concentrated, if I gathered all my will and invested it in making that package disappear, maybe, *maybe* it wouldn't exist. But it was still there. I caved at the evidence that there was no turning back and carefully removed the paper. Carlos hugged me from behind, his chin resting on my shoulder, watching as I unwrapped and opened the box.

There was my doll. Resting on cardboard. He didn't even bother to give her a proper bed. Under it, he at least had the decency to leave a note.

EVA: Do you remember what it said?

CORAL: As if I were reading it now. I read it so many times I learned it by heart. "My Torment, it is impossible for me to stay close to you when our love is impossible. They will never let us be together, so it is better for both of us that I leave. Be very happy, be an extraordinary woman. Maybe someday I'll learn to forget you. I love you."

EVA: It does not appear in the trial documentation.

CORAL: No. Ayalga made me swallow it.

CORAL

I let Carlos take care of the doll and ran up the road to Raúl's house.

It was empty. Looking through the windows, there was nothing left of him inside. He had gone and left me alone. Ayalga had promised. I had done my part, and Raúl was gone. He was going to love me forever, but away from me? What was the point of that? Tears wouldn't let me see clearly. My throat twisted as if someone had put a noose around my neck as I hurried to my forest with the note clutched in one hand and Güelita's knitting needles in the other. I wasn't about to let her fool me.

"You promised," I protested from under the branches of the oak tree. "We made a deal and you tricked me. What is this supposed to be? If Raúl's not going to be with me, you won't have ANYTHING either."

I nailed the note to the trunk with one of the needles. Blood blossomed on the page as if I had stabbed myself with it. I screamed in desperation, hating her with all my soul as I lay down on the branches and threw my underwear as far away as I could. I knew it was going to hurt, but I didn't care at all. Pain was already flooding my soul, it couldn't get any worse. I spread my legs and prepared to stick the knitting needle inside me, to kill the creature nesting there, when thick, hard roots came out of the ground and held my hands so tightly I had no choice but to let go. I thought she would break my wrists.

The ground between my legs opened up. The light of the forest became bluish and faint. The wind was shaking the branches of the oak tree with such force it seemed as if it would tear all the leaves off. Ayalga's eyes, now completely black instead of green, watched me over my pubis. The roots loosened the tension, and I was able to pull back, close my legs and lean against the bark of the tree as she clung to the earth and climbed out of it.

"What did you intend to do, my sweet girl?" Her voice sounded hoarse, deep as thunder, echoing in my head and all around me.

"You tricked me. You lied to me," I managed to answer, although my voice was barely a whisper. I pulled Raúl's note out of the bark. "Raúl has abandoned me."

The trunk of the tree became a sticky mass, like the day Olvido had rested her hand on it, sinking into my back with unimaginable pain. It trapped and immobilized me. It made me understand there were worse sufferings than that of the heart, that scorched flesh can make us give in. Ayalga pounced on me. Her body seemed much bigger. Full of cutting edges. The mushrooms on her breasts were red and mottled. From the moss on her pubis and head protruded eager vipers and tiny vermin. With her elongated, sharp fingers she opened my mouth. I tried to resist and only succeeded in getting cuts on my cheeks and lips. I gave in when the familiar taste of blood reached my tongue. She placed the paper with Raúl's note on it and closed my mouth again. I chewed the paper mixed with my own blood as I had done so many other times with the oak leaves. The salt of my tears seeped between my lips as she held my jaw shut, pinning her round, black rodent eyes to mine.

"Distance only makes love grow stronger, child. We're just making sure you won't leave, that you won't take our baby with you. Raúl will come back when I hold her in my arms."

I managed to swallow Raúl's words. The light shone through the branches again. The wind stopped and I fell forward into Ayalga's arms as the oak trunk released my back now full of splinters. She had regained the softness, the gentleness, and dried my tears.

"That's it, my sweet girl, that's it," she said, cradling me. "I'll take care of you, and Raúl will be back."

I closed my eyes and let her rock me to sleep.

Hiding my pregnancy wasn't hard. No one gave a shit. Guillermo would have had to look at me more than twice to realize I had put on weight. In high school I wore baggy sweatshirts and scarves. I didn't let Tony touch me, so he wouldn't have noticed either. Ayalga took care of the baby and me. I would lie naked on the roots, my belly bulging, watching the movements under my skin. I would tilt my head back and the xana would lie on top of me. She opened her mouth and poured her saliva, her sap, her brown blood made of earth and water into my mouth. I have never encountered such a taste again. It made my whole body vibrate, I was on the verge of orgasm just by the simple act of swallowing and the creature writhed inside me, rejoicing.

I began to feel what, according to the Internet, were the first signs of labor on the eve of Epiphany. It was a sign. Ayalga and I had met that day eight years before. A lifetime. Hiding my pregnancy under my huge sweatshirt and with a backpack on my back, trying to look as normal as possible, I told Guillermo I was going for a walk.

Carlos and Señor Magia wanted to follow me, but I gave them both a kiss and asked for a time alone. This moment was for the oak tree and myself. Pain was already conquering every inch of my body as I entered the forest at dusk. In the village everyone would be enjoying the Reyes Magos parade. Too happy and too busy.

The forest greeted me with golden light, warmth and the smell of flowers. I thought it was the best way for my baby to come into this world. Although, in reality, she wasn't going to be mine, was she? I had promised her long ago. I sat on the ground, my back against the bark of the oak tree. She sat across from me.

"Open your mouth, my sweet girl," she murmured.

As always, I did as I was commanded. Ayalga then caressed my tongue with her long, blackish, sharp fingers. I closed my eyes. Although her fingers resembled oak branches, they were soft and slimy like slugs on my tongue. They invaded me with a bitter taste, but when she made me close my mouth and swallow, the pain was completely gone. As if it had never been there.

It wasn't easy to do it all on my own with the only help of my cell phone, a video tutorial and what my body knew was right, pain free. But I did it. The forest took care of it. I concentrated on the wind passing through the branches of the trees, singing me a lullaby, on the feel of the grass in my hands. Ayalga would protect me and our baby.

I squatted down and hugged my knees. The xana was sitting in front of me, squeezing my belly. A little girl fell to the ground between my legs.

She smelled like vanilla.

I should have noticed.

I should have been smarter.

My baby was not covered in fungus and moss. She didn't even look like the xana. She was like any other human newborn, wrapped in white mucus and blood, she stretched out her arms and opened her mouth to cry, to breathe air for the first time, but determined to get Raúl back, I put my hand over the baby's mouth and nose. I squeezed as Ayalga looked up at me smiling, opening her arms to welcome the baby into her kingdom. Ants and snails, worms and beetles climbed up my hands and slipped into her mouth as I squeezed.

And I squeezed.

The pink skin turned blue.

The baby was nothing more than an empty, warm sock under my hands. Just like my hamster had been the night it all began. Ayalga kissed me on the mouth. We had come full circle. The journey was over. I tasted my freedom for the first time on her cat tongue. I kissed the still-warm baby on the forehead.

"See you soon."

"She will be happy here with me, better than with any of you humans," Ayalga murmured, welcoming my child into the tree trunk. As soon as it began to close around her, I could hear the baby take a big breath and cry. Tears of joy and relief streamed down my face.

I listened to the baby's cries that crept through the branches and turned into distant whistles. Into the song of the birds. She was the murmur of the insects around me. The sunlight between the branches.

I buried the placenta and tried to clean myself. The anesthetic effect of Ayalga's touch was dissipating. The forest light was no longer golden. Cold. An icy wind blew through the now leafless branches of the oak tree. The world around me had changed. My forest was no longer a forest. It was nothing more than a patch of dry land populated by rickety trees and hungry squirrels staring at me in fright.

I had given it all away, my last drop of magic, of love, of myself. Now Raúl would come back. She had promised. Till death do us part. That was the deal. He was going to be mine until his heart stopped beating. Because if this wasn't love for life, the kind of love that defies death, then I would have been just a toy in Raúl's hands. I would have been nothing more than a cliché. An imbecile who falls in love with a teacher and lets herself be fooled. I buried my underwear and the towels I used to clean myself and returned home hoping only one night would separate me from the Prince Charming I deserved.

I confessed during the trial, but my child is not dead. She is not. But how could anyone believe me if they couldn't hear my baby in the air. Smell her in the mushrooms, and in the forest soil. You have to believe, to see.

VOICE NOTE FROM ESTELA GOMEZ ON JENNIFER PELAEZ'S ANSWERING MA- CHINE

Dated January 5, 2019

I'm convinced, Jenni. Eva wouldn't have hanged herself without seeing the little girl, without being able to handle the last episode of the podcast. Without saying goodbye to Coral. It's absurd. I knew I was right.

Eva committed suicide to protect me, to protect the child. Can't you see that? I have left you in the post office box an envelope with the memory cards and the notes I have taken during these months. If I don't come back, if we don't come back, there you have it all.

I'm going to fix it. I'm going to fix everything.

And I'm going to bring Eva back.

CORAL

It was Epiphany and I was going to receive my most precious gift. My body was raw from the night before. My
belly, empty, still bulged and everything hurt. It hurt to walk,
to urinate. It radiated from my sex but spread like roots all over
my body. My breasts, full of life and milk, were yearning for the
baby's mouth. I squeezed them in the shower and watched the
white liquid ooze from them, relieving the pressure. I believed
Ayalga's word so much that I imagined myself having breakfast
with Guillermo, Carlos and Señor Magia. Opening presents
together as if we were a family again. I thought Olvido and
Marisa would also return. I had given her what she wanted, the
biggest sacrifice of all.

Shouldn't she be grateful?

The house was awfully quiet. Downstairs the light seemed
bluer than usual. More silent. Suspended. The air was too frigid
even for January. I breathed in and a soft smell of disturbed earth

and dampness filled my lungs. It should have smelled like fresh coffee and churros. I was not prepared for what awaited me.

I went downstairs and the scent was unbearable. A putrid odor coated with a metallic tinge that clung to my tongue. The kitchen lights were off. Flour and sugar scattered all over the countertop, mixed with a muddy liquid that dripped to the floor. The faucet was running. I walked over to the sink to turn it off.

Under the table with the old Christmas tree, right where I had hidden when I was eight years old, lay Guillermo surrounded by presents. Bitten. Bloodied. Blue. His eyes wide and watery. His expression was void. He was nothing more than an empty carcass. I knelt beside him. He was still warm to the touch. His blood was still liquid. I kissed his forehead and realized at that moment how unfair I had been to him. In an instant I had an idea. I would take my father's still warm corpse into the forest. She would bring him back. I had to do it. I owed it to myself.

"I'll bring you back, *Dad*," the word strange on my tongue. A chestnut bur I was trying to swallow whole.

I yelled for Carlos and Señor Magia to assist. Dad was too heavy. I could barely lift him halfway off the floor. My brother and my dog didn't come to the call. I screamed again with tears choking my throat, my voice breaking, but still no response.

Covered in my father's blood, I went outside. I could not believe my eyes.

Raúl, my Raúl, the love of my short life was there in my backyard, though it wasn't exactly what I had asked for or expected. Raúl, my Raúl, my love, was at my feet devouring Señor Magia on the porch. Tearing skin and flesh with each desperate bite. The dog, still alive, looked at me, and tried to move, I felt his desperation to protect me, but then all the light in his eyes faded, and the fur turned to moss. His bright red blood turned to brown mud with an earthy smell. His bones were branches sticking out of the grass. Señor Magia's belly burst like a bag of thick white worms writhing around taking the life from inside him back to the earth, back to the forest.

I stepped back and tried not to make a sound. He was not the man I had asked for. Had I not made the greatest sacrifice of all, only to find myself betrayed like this by Ayalga?

In the middle of the courtyard, Carlos lay with an open bite on his neck. He was trying to speak but could not. He had also been beaten. Torn by the mimic that was my dead lover. His blood was not blood at all, but a slow river of earth returning to earth, just like Señor Magia.

Only then did the weight of my actions make me scream. The image of my mother running away from the house came to mind. She had seen it. So had Aunt Olvido. They saw. And now their bodies were sticking out of the grass in the garden. The roots of the trees expelled them, they no longer needed them, they repudiated them. In the frenzy of what was happening I could recognize their clothes. Their half-rotten faces. Olvido's black hair.

As Carlos and Señor Magia dissolved into the illusion they were, I knew I had killed my brother. I had killed the hamster. The little bird. Their corpses were still rotting in the place where I had buried them.

Raúl heard my startled cry as my hip hit the back door. The torrent of emotions oozed from my eyes in cascades. He let go of the dog and looked at me. His face was not the dreamscape I had kissed and longed for. The face I had imagined when I smothered her baby. It was nothing but a jumble of maggot-filled dog bites. His shirt was covered in dried blood and dirt. His curly hair was dry. He smiled at me with a rotten mouth, missing teeth here and there, dangling over a black tongue. His smile was crooked. He winked at me or did a bad imitation of a wink with lidless eyes, as he had done that first day when I imagined he was going to suffer an episode of spontaneous combustion.

Raúl, or at least, what Ayalga was willing to give me, groped me. His cold fingers clung against the bare skin of my arms. The still tender flesh of my body ached. I escaped his attempted embrace and ran down the three steps of the deck to my brother whose blood was not crimson, but dark chocolate. He smelled of earth. His skin turned to wood. His hair into grass. He was melting into the earth as Señor Magia had done.

Before I could react, Raúl jumped out of the deck. He grabbed me and forced me back upstairs. He pushed me against the wall, like he had done that night outside his window. Raúl was showing me all his rotten love by suffocating me in his stench of death. My back was against the wood of the fence surrounding the house. His embrace was too strong. There was no escape. Maybe some other time, when my whole body didn't ache from childbirth and my soul didn't ache with the realization of my crimes. Of my losses.

Everything ached as he pressed his broken ribs against my flesh. The skin cracked, staining my Christmas pajamas with roses of blood. Opening wounds that filled my lungs with fluid. My chest constricted as the blood wouldn't let any more air in.

He kissed me. I coughed. The maggots from Raúl's face wriggled into my mouth. I choked on them. With my own blood. I couldn't breathe.

Christmas lights twinkled above my head as Raúl's hands reached under my pajamas and caressed my breasts that dripped milk over the blood soaking my camisole. There was only one thing I could do to survive. I burrowed my hands into his open ribcage, ripping the remaining flesh from his body. I tore it open and clutched his cold heart. It was almost black, shining through the open wound. Too tender. I could feel maggots moving inside it. A steady rhythm of sap flowing through its cavities, mimicking life. I crushed it as hard as I suffocated the hamster. Like my granny to the pigeons for rice. *They don't suffer, they don't suffer, they don't suffer…*

His body fell to the ground. Hollow.

Until his heart stopped beating. That was not what I wished for.

And now you tell me he's still alive?

So, Ayalga still owes me a debt. For years, I have suffocated in this asylum surrounded by asphalt, without trees, without forest, without the murmur of the river. Trapped far away from her. How would she find a way to me if it hadn't been for you?

Right now, as we speak, Raúl is drowning in his cell, in a black vomit of churned earth and white maggots, and she is here with me again. You have brought me this breath of fresh air and, not only that. A name. A certainty. This time Ayalga has promised to give me what I want, the revenge I deserve. The freedom I deserve. To fly, again. I hope you can forgive me for what I've done to you, Eva. You can't stop her now.

I'm sorry.

260 J.V. GACHS

ESTELA

I struggle to force my belly under the broken wire fence. We've been together forty weeks now. *A Christmas child.* The first thing you said when we calculated the day I would be due. Now I understand the excitement. Now I know that feeling wasn't yours. Or at least, not entirely.

It is January 5th.

It is the night of Epiphany.

It's been six months since you hanged from that tree and there's still a piece of the police cordon they used to keep on-lookers away from your flailing body. The air should be cold. It was stormy when I got off the freeway, but the temperature has risen since I got in here. From the outside it seemed smaller. Dry. Now, surrounded by the trees and fireflies, the branches are covered with green leaves. The moon is full although it shouldn't be. I look up at the sky and make out constellations that make no sense in this place, at this time of year. Everything is as Coral described it.

The child stirs uneasily inside my womb. This spawn whose heart does not beat but who lives inside me. I run my hand over my belly, while a soft wind sneaks through the branches of the trees and ruffles my hair. It is warm. I take off my jacket and throw it on the ground covered with fresh grass and daisies.

I hum a sweet lullaby. A chorus of nocturnal animals accompanies me with their whistling.

It smells like vanilla.

It's not hard to follow the path to the oak tree. My heart is about to burst. My breathing quickens. The girl batters my ribs, I don't know if with her fists or her feet. I notice how she tries to turn inside me. As if she wanted to run away. Whether from me or from what lives in the forest remains to be seen.

I try to imagine you walking this path with us. Your hand intertwined with mine. Your smile. But with every step, the image that pops into my head like flowers blooming is the twisted grimace of your face inside the box. The absurd makeup that attempted to remove the obvious signs of death on your face.

You, who never wore makeup. You looked like a sad, dead clown laying there with your eyes closed. I wondered if your eyes were red from lack of oxygen. Full of little spots of blood from burst capillaries. I stop for a second, sigh and close my eyes.

I have finally arrived under the oak tree. The girl scratches my belly from the inside when I reach my hand to the trunk of the tree. A light caress makes my skin crawl as if a butterfly had flown past my neck. I turn around but I'm still alone.

I put the backpack on the ground and take out your ashes. I pick them up and turn around.

Come on, I think restlessly, I *know you're here*.

I focus on you, Eva. Your body on the white satin of the box, painted like a buffoon. Your back walking out the door with your wallet crossed over your chest and the tape recorder in your pocket. Your lips kissing my belly the day the test came back positive. Naked next to me in bed, asleep covered in sweat. Kissing my chin. Moaning. Licking me. You. The love, the desire, the need to get you back, that suffocating feeling that there would be nothing, NOTHING, I wouldn't be willing to give to kiss you again. To give life to your heart. To make you breathe again.

Her presence suddenly invades everything. Her breath, almost a laugh, suspended behind my neck.

"Ah, finally, there you are." I feel rough hands like tree bark stroking my belly under my clothes. "You and I are going to make a deal."

EPILOGUE

Excerpt from THE GARDEN OF HORRORS: A True Crime Company Podcast

Episode 1 Season 2, aired on June 1, 2019

[The Bear Dance, acoustic version]

Hello, *gardeners*, I am Noelia Urzaiz, your new host on this season of every sleuth's favorite podcast, The Garden of Horrors. One year after our first season turned into a phenomenon online, we are back with a brand-new investigation. In this season's ten episodes, we will unravel the crimes of Dolores Álvarez-Quintana. But before we dive into that, we want to give you all some updates from the previous case. You won't stop clogging our social media with the latest rumors, so here it is. Everything we know so far:▯

Raúl Expósito, Coral's teacher, was found dead in his cell the same day our colleague Eva Villar hanged herself in the woods. We only learned about this because we tried to contact him again to get a statement after our last episode aired. We figured the podcast's success would make him more willing to talk. The cause of death was filed as *natural*, cardiac arrest.

From what we've been told, an autopsy was not performed, and his body was cremated soon after. However, an anonymous source, an eyewitness, has shared with us a *slightly* different opinion about the cause of death. Here's a fragment of the email we got:▯

"I've seen many dead people in my years here. Some inmates can't deal with life anymore and kill themselves, and they can get really creative about that if you'll take my word for it. Fights, diseases…

But I've never EVER seen anything like that. He was found naked on the floor; his expression was that of sheer horror. He had tried to blind himself with his bare hands. His face was full of scratches and dried blood. His whole body looked as if he had been rubbing his skin against blackberry bushes or barbwire. There was mud stuffed in his mouth. I don't have the faintest idea of how he could get a hold of that many leaves, twigs, and that much earth as we found under his corpse. I mean, we are surrounded by parking lots and concrete and buildings, not even a small park nearby. That awful chocolate paste was dripping from his open mouth as if it came from his insides. There's not a night I don't see that man's corpse in my mind when I close my eyes. Whatever it was, it was a horrible, HORRIBLE way to go. And it didn't make any sense to investigate the thing further, you see, he was locked inside alone. However creative his death was, he did it to himself. It was just easier for everybody to look the other way, just cremate him, and be done with it. No one cared anyway."

Also, as you all may know, Coral López Ramos escaped the Corazón de María six months ago, just after Epiphany. She was doing some gardening, surrounded by doctors and other patients, they blinked, and she was gone. Her escape was immediately reported, but by the time police officers got there she was nowhere to be found. It was as if she had taken flight. An investigation into her escape is currently ongoing although it seems pretty clear there are no viable leads for the police to follow. Coral vanished into thin air in the middle of the day, in plain sight, leaving nothing but questions behind.

A little birdie told us that, as of right now, police might be looking for a body and not a fugitive. Said birdie hasn't disclosed with us the reasons yet, though.▯

We don't like to speculate. This is a serious podcast where we love facts and these are the facts: Everyone involved in the gruesome crimes of Coral López Ramos or their investigation for this podcast is now either dead or presumed dead. There's no way to prove foul play. There're no more threads to pull from. From now on, until a new piece of evidence is unearthed, or a witness comes forward, your guess of what really happened is as good as ours.▨

But don't despair, we have many *facts* to share with you about our new case. Was Dolores Álvarez-Quintana a cold-blooded murderer, a mentally ill woman or was she possessed? This season in the Garden of Horrors: Next Door Devil.

QUICK Favor

Thank you so much for dedicating your time to reading this book! May we ask a quick favor?

Will you please take a moment to leave a review on Amazon, Goodreads, or wherever you purchased the book? Your words have power. Your review can help this book reach more readers. We appreciate you!

Acknowledgements

I can only start this by thanking my father, Manuel, for working hard away from home so I could have all the opportunities; and my mother, Julia Cecilia, for staying home away from the love of her life to take care of me and for nurturing my soul with books. And Juan who endures, patiently, my rambling about plot.

Huge thanks to Patrick Barb for being the closest thing to a mentor I can think of. To Saúl Montes for lending me his journalist brain to write the news articles in here. And Lidia López for beta reading it. To Sarah Barter for editing my first short stories, giving me the confidence to keep on writing in English.

To Jorge, Inés, Irma, David, Luisje e Iria for being the best writing squad I could ask for. To A.P. Thayer for his patience and the encouragement.

Finally, my immense gratitude to L.C. Marino and L.P. Hernandez for giving this story a new opportunity and to Yorgos Cotronis for bringing my xana to life in the cover.

More great titles from Sobelo Books
available at www.SobeloBooks.com
and wherever books are sold.